CW01677280

for Rebekah -
many thanks
for your help!

Enjoy!

Naomi H.

THE SECRET

By Naomi Hudson

Also by the author

Bluebell
A romantic quest, published in 2015.

Aphrodite's Curse
A tale of seduction and murder published in 2016.

Snow Maiden,
A tale of romance, betrayal & violence, published in 2017.

The Golden Chrysanthemums
The hunt for a serial killer in Whitby, published in 2018.

The Secret
is her fifth novel.

All are mainly set in Yorkshire. The characters of Bentley and Ryan appear in the last four books.

THE SECRET

By Naomi Hudson

Published in 2019

ISBN: 978-1-9160217-5-4

Book interior & Cover Design/Photography
by Russell Holden
www.pixeltweakspublications.com

Pixel Tweaks Publications
SELF-PUBLISHING MADE SIMPLE

www.varykinocollectables.co.uk

Find Naomi Hudson on Facebook

This book is dedicated to three of my oldest and dearest friends, George, Lionel, and Jenny who all passed away in January 2019.

Map of North Yorkshire

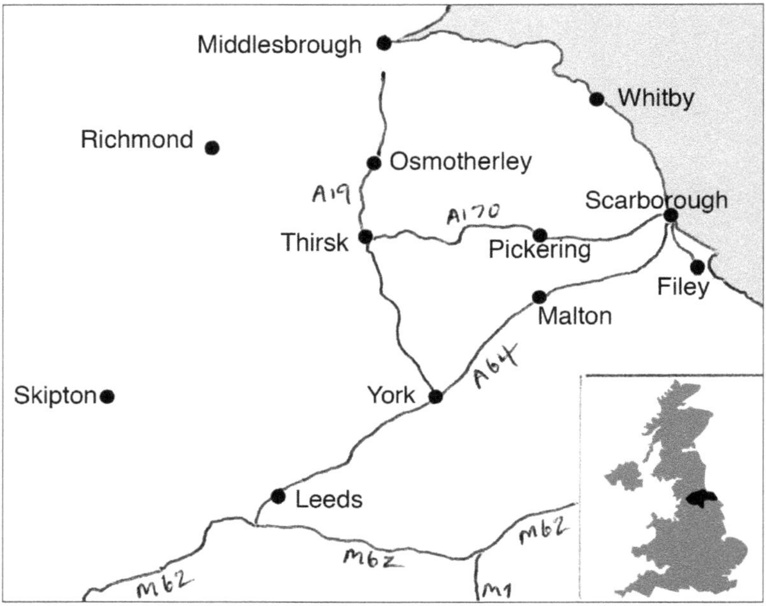

• PART ONE •

CHAPTER ONE

Tiny splashes of snow still clung to the hedgerows, but elsewhere patches of green, young shoots, were promising the arrival of an early spring. It had rained during the afternoon, leaving shallow puddles on the driveway, but now the night air had become chilly, with the clearing sky threatening a brief frost. An occasional cloud masked the crescent moon, as the dark figure made his way along the edge of the driveway, pausing here and there as a sudden noise made him freeze and merge into the darkness.

There had been a mansion here once, one of those elegant Victorian structures built for a Bradford cotton merchant, but the estate had decayed during the 1920s. The house had been used by the military during the War, but the soldiers treated the house as a rough billet, leaving it to deteriorate further, and in 1958 the Council took over the estate and demolished the main buildings, just leaving stone gateposts and sections of garden walls standing like gravestones, reminders of what had once been. "We've created a new park for local people to enjoy," one of the councillors stated,

"Abbotsfield, *somewhere nice in the country where folk can walk and enjoy the fresh air." A few large boulders were placed creatively on one of the former lawns, but the rest of the estate, once proud gardens and orchards, was allowed to gradually die and become overgrown. The grounds became choked with brambles, with just a few narrow paths for children to explore and for dogs to chase rabbits.*

The man continued to make his way along the former driveway, as it twisted towards the grounds of the ruined mansion. He was dressed entirely in black, and he now moved more quickly as the chill increased. He had work to do. He was carrying a package over his left shoulder, a wrapped tapering package that would have resembled a rifle or shotgun to anyone who spotted him, but he was sure that no-one would see him. He also had a short trench spade in his right hand. He continued moving silently, glancing around from time to time, and pausing, listening ... still no-one around. As he approached the former lawns, he found a path on the right and pushed his way past some trees and through some brambles until he reached the back of the old orchard, about thirty yards away from the old driveway. He knew where he was going. Two or three mounds were close to the former garden wall, and he moved round the back of the middle mound, pausing for a minute or two before laying down the package then carefully digging into the mound on the left side. It was tiring work. The ground was still hard under the surface, but he took his time, piling up the soil by the wall, and wiping the sweat from his forehead.

He continued digging, then lifted the package to the narrow trench he had created to check that it would fit. He placed the package to one side, and carried on, lengthening the trench, then adding more depth. It was now slow progress, and the man sat back on one of the other mounds, wiping away the sweat again and breathing heavily. He glanced above, where the clouds had parted, lightening the grounds with shafts of moonlight.

A bark! The man froze, then slowly eased himself to the top of the mound and peered through the trees towards the tumble of boulders on the former lawn. He squinted. A small terrier dashed across the lawn, sniffed around one of the boulders, then scurried away into the undergrowth on the other side of the lawn. A minute later the dog reappeared, and the man ducked down. "Bouncer...Bouncer!" A woman's voice from the driveway. "Bouncer, get over here!" she ordered. More barking, then the sound of quiet voices, then nothing. The man began to ease himself back up the mound, then he heard some laughter. He froze again, waiting for the silence to return. A few minutes later, he moved to the top of the mound and squinted at the boulders. The dog was lying down, with its lead fastened around one of the smaller rocks. A young woman, naked to the waist, was sitting on the edge of one of the flatter boulders, the moonlight reflecting on her breasts, as a man pulled down her jeans then unzipped his fly. The chill gave an urgency to their lovemaking. He eased her up slightly, then entered her quickly, as she wrapped her arms around his neck. The dog sat up, whimpering, as their movements quickened, the woman gasping as the thrusts pushed her onto her back, trying to grip the boulder. The man climaxed, and their movements slowed, calmer now, as she stood up and kissed him. "Christ, it's bloody freezing," she exclaimed, breaking away from him and dressing quickly. The man helped her on with her top, and then handed over her coat. "I'm shivering, Paul," she spoke more loudly, glancing around belatedly, "come on, let's go." She bent down to pick up the dog's lead, then, hand in hand, the couple began walking briskly, laughing, looking back at the boulders, until they melted into the shadows.

The man in black waited for a few minutes, then stood up and peered back at the driveway. Silence again. He glanced upwards as the clouds began to return, masking the moon, then he looked down at the trench. He removed a little more earth from the edges, then lifted the package and forced it into the trench, packing the earth around it, adding more soil, then packing again, making sure that the trench was solid. He continued working until the mound was smooth, then he dragged some thin branches and brambles onto the mound, trying to make sure that the trench was hidden. He stepped back, then used his spade to scatter the remaining soil over the former garden wall, or into the tangles of brambles that surrounded him. He felt around on the ground to make sure that the loose soil had been cleared, then, glancing around, he made his way back along the path to the old driveway.

It was now after midnight, very quiet, quite dark, as he reached the lane at the end of the driveway and walked quickly down the hill, hugging the wall, looking for the small clearing where he had parked his car. Opening the door, he removed his shoes and gloves and put them in a carrier bag, to be dumped in someone's bin on the way home. "Four down, two to go," he muttered to himself, then he closed the door and drove off into the darkness.

CHAPTER TWO

Turn back the clock. Saturday 13 December, 1997. Phoebe Bartlett was beginning to get annoyed. She glanced at her watch, then pushed back hard against the wall of the Stephen Joseph Theatre on Northway, adjusting her umbrella as a drip caught the shoulder of her coat. It was a foul evening, and Phoebe's temper was about to match it. She glared at a couple of theatregoers as the man briefly stared at her as they rushed by on their way to the entrance to the theatre, then she checked her watch again. *Where the fuck is he?* she thought, glancing up and down the street, then flicking a few raindrops from her face.

Phoebe was used to men staring at her, in fact she quite enjoyed it, confident in the knowledge that, at 42, she still could turn a man's head. Good-looking, blonde-haired, smartly-dressed, and statuesque – Phoebe was a very attractive lady with the figure of a woman ten years younger than herself. She was a good catch and she knew it, which was one of the reasons why her patience was wearing thin. *I'll give him five more minutes,* she decided, as another man gawped at her, then she turned away and looked at her watch again. She was putting her hands into her pockets when a battered BMW convertible roared around the corner by the station and screetched to a halt by the kerbside. A tall, dark-haired young man got out of the driver's door and began to edge round the front of the car.

"Phoebe", be began apologetically, "I'm …"

"Get back in," she hissed at him, glancing back towards the entrance as a camera flashed in the shadows, and reaching for the door handle. She eased into the front seat, her long legs dangling for a few seconds as the camera flashed again, then she slammed the door. "Get me away from here, Jack," she muttered as he opened his mouth to speak. "Move it!" The car roared off along Northway, turned right into Victoria Road and disappeared from view.

***

A pale light filtered into the room from the kitchen. Jack moved slightly away from Phoebe on the bed and sat up, the perspiration glistening on his forehead as he ran his fingers through her hair. He leant forward and kissed her, then collapsed onto his back. "Jesus, Phoebe, you're a top woman. You were fantastic!" She moved slightly and placed her hand on his chest.

"I'm always fantastic," she spoke slowly, smiling, "and don't you forget it!" Jack could see her white teeth in the gloom. "You're not too bad … getting better, I'd say." He laughed, and they clung together for a minute or two, before he eased them both to a sitting position against the bedhead. Jack looked down, then back at Phoebe, who was relaxing more after their frantic lovemaking, her breasts rising and falling more slowly now.

"I'm really sorry about before, Phoebe … you know, being late, but our coach broke down after leaving Scunthorpe." He smiled briefly. "I was in such a great mood after the match. We won, I scored twice, and now I'm the leading scorer in the league. I just wanted to get back here as quickly as possible, to tell you about the match, and to share some quality time with you, but then…"

"Don't worry, pet, I was angry earlier on, but now I know that it wasn't your fault. These things happen," she muttered, moving over to kiss him, then turning around to face him, "but make sure that it doesn't happen again!" She smiled again, then frowned as she glanced down at her watch. "Look, Jack, we don't have much more time tonight, so listen, please. Call me on Wednesday, and I'll tell you where to meet me next Saturday night. Don't be late this time," she glared at him, then smiled, "because I've something special lined up for you!"

"Have I got to wait that long?" he grinned, reaching forward and caressing her left breast.

"That's nice," she whispered, placing her hand over his, then she quickly moved to the edge of the bed and stood up, tall in the half-light. "Yes, you do have to bloody wait, Lover Boy!" Jack smiled, admiring the outline of her full figure, then shifted off the bed, stood up and wrapped his arms around her.

"I'll phone you next Wednesday afternoon, after training," he laughed softly. "Your surprise had better be worth waiting for."

***

Dennis Slater manoeuvred his tray of coffees around a couple of PCs and headed for the CID room, where Debbie Chapman and George Ryan were chatting quietly and Tim Sharpe, his feet resting on his desk, was reading the Scarborough Evening News. "Lucky bastard!" he exclaimed loudly.

"What's up now, Sharpie?" Slater asked, as he handed a mug to Chapman. Ryan reached for another. "Well?" Slater muttered again, as he peered over Sharpe's shoulder and placed a mug on his desk.

"Look at this, Dennis," Sharpe grunted, handing him the open paper and pointing at a headline:

SEADOGS STRIKER SCORES AGAIN … AND AGAIN!

Popular Scarborough FC striker Jack Mason struck two more goals against Scunthorpe United on Saturday afternoon, then celebrated with a stunning mystery blonde during the evening. Our cameraman snapped the long-legged beauty as she eased into Mason's BMW convertible near the Stephen Joseph Theatre …

Slater glanced at the three photos alongside the article, showing Jack Mason in his football kit, a blurred shot of Phoebe turning, and a flurry of legs in the passenger seat of his car.

"Like I said, Dennis … lucky bastard. I bet he's shagging a different bird every weekend." He paused in thought. "I was pretty good at football at school. I should have stuck with it," he muttered, gazing again at the photos.

"You're just like a football, Sharpie," the dark-haired Debbie Chapman called across the room, "full of wind." The others laughed, then turned as Sharpe swung his legs off the table.

"Afternoon, Boss," he spluttered.

"What's the big joke?" Bentley asked.

"It's Sharpie as usual, Sir," Chapman grinned, "thinks he would have made a great footballer and scored with loads of women."

"Really," Bentley smiled, "or perhaps he would have enjoyed the big bath with the rest of the lads!" Laughter.

"No way," gasped a red-faced Sharpe, turning around to glance at George Ryan. "That's not my scene."

"Right, Christmas may be just around the corner,“ Bentley grunted sternly, "but I think you've all got something better to do than play party games. Let's get down to it." He watched as order was restored. "George … have you got a minute?" Ryan followed the DI into his office near the doorway. "Don't look so worried, George," Bentley smiled. "Jean was wondering what you are doing for Christmas. She's worried that you'll be spending it alone in your flat, and so she wants you to know that you're welcome to come along to our house for Christmas dinner … turkey and all the trimmings."

"That's really kind of you, Sir … and it would be lovely, but I usually return to Darlington to do the family thing, you know, catch up with relatives and eat too much." He smiled briefly. "I think my mother would be upset if I don't show my face."

"Good, that's fine, George. I can reassure Jean that you won't be languishing on your tod." He paused, then added. "You've had a stressful few months, lad, but I'm pleased that you've come through it. You may be quiet, but I think you're made of pretty stern stuff." He ushered Ryan towards the door. "If anything changes …"

"Thanks, Sir."

***

Phoebe Bartlett wrapped herself in a pale lilac towel, then entered the bedroom and lay down beside Jack Mason. Scarborough FC had played a home match against Barnet on Friday evening, so Phoebe had booked the Plough Hotel near Pickering, and the couple were able to spend a romantic weekend together. They shared a shower on this Sunday morning following an evening of passion and an early-morning session of lovemaking. Phoebe ran her fingers through the mass of dark hair on Jack's chest, then nudged him as he began to nod off.

"Lightweight," she whispered, laughing softly as he imitated a victim who had just been tortured on the rack. "I thought you footballers were supposed to be fit!"

"I am, Phoebe, but I wasn't expecting another hard training session after playing a match on Friday night," he joked. "Next time, can we just go for a quiet meal, or have some popcorn at the pictures?"

"Oh, poor tired little Jack," she taunted, caressing him again. "Next time I'll bring you a pipe and some slippers!" They both laughed and cuddled each other, until Phoebe noticed that he was getting aroused and she sat up on her pillow. "Now listen Jack, before we head for extra time, it's Christmas soon, then New Year, so I won't be able to see for a couple of weeks or so. My family has a lot of traditions … parties, visits to long-lost relatives, big meals … you know, too much going on. You understand, don't you?" He grimaced, looking down, then reached for her. "We wouldn't be able to have any quality time together, and anyway you'll be busy with more training and matches … and lots of travelling."

"OK, Phoebe, you're right as usual, I suppose."

"I'm not going to run away, Jack, or to disappear into the sunset," she smiled as he pretended to pout. "We'll have plenty of time to catch up next year, won't we?"

"Yeah, next year's going to be great."

CHAPTER THREE

George Ryan paused, skimmed the last few sentences he had typed, then glanced out of the window. It was drizzling slightly. Christmas, he thought to himself, just around the corner. Back to Darlington for a few days, too much family and too much to eat. It could have been so different if things had worked out with Fiona. The rain intensified. He frowned, then jumped as Debbie touched his shoulder. "Sorry, Debbie," he muttered, smiling briefly, "I was miles away."

"Coffee then?" Ryan nodded. "It might wake you up, George." She moved off, asking the others if they wanted a drink. Ryan looked back at the report he was writing, gathered his thoughts, then began tapping the keyboard again. A prolific shoplifter had been arrested again the previous week. Waste of time, he'll get another rap on the knuckles, then carry on stealing until the next time. He thought about the next section of his report, then tapped in a few more words, sitting back as Debbie arrived with a drink.

"Thanks, Debbie," he smiled at her, then sipping the drink and pulling a face as it was too hot. He was longing to ask her about Fiona, who had moved in with Debbie the previous October, but as before he said nothing and neither did she. Debbie had moved on to Tim Sharpe's desk, and was chatting to him. Sharpe was the joker in the pack, a sarcastic individual who often used Ryan as the butt of his humour. For the past month or so, however, Sharpe had been more serious than usual.

"How's Laura, Tim, and her little bump?" Debbie asked.

"Laura's fine, Debs, thanks for asking, and the little bump is not so little!" They both laughed.

"When's the big day, Sharpie?" Dennis Slater asked. He was the quiet researcher in the team.

"Eighteenth of January, give or take. I don't know much about these things," he said, shrugging his shoulders, "but all of Laura's scans have been fine, so I hope everything continues to go smoothly until the little one arrives." The others smiled, and Ryan stopped working.

"Where's the Boss, Debbie? It's not like him to be so late," he said.

"I received a note to say that he would be late in," replied Debbie, "but I don't know why."

"He's probably gone to Whitby for some of his precious jelly-babies," Sharpe quipped, and the others laughed again. The small chat continued for a few minutes until the door opened, and a grim-faced DI Bentley marched in. He glanced at the anxious faces around the room, walked up to his desk, draped his jacket around his chair, then perched on the edge of his desk.

"You've probably been wondering why I'm so late?" he asked, looking from face to face. "Well I can tell you that I've been on the phone to the Chief Constable," he added, continuing to look bullish, "to tell him about this." He brandished a greetings card in his right hand, looking again at the puzzled faces in front of him, then he dropped in onto the desk. "It's a Christmas card," he explained solemnly, then his face broke into a broad grin, "and it's only from our Maddie!" There was a second or two of silence as the team took in the DI's message, then smiles appeared. "Our Maddie," Bentley was still grinning as he lifted the card again, "she's bloody alive and living in Ireland." Suddenly everyone was on their feet, and they crowded around Bentley, shaking his hand, then Debbie gave him a big hug. Bentley waited for the noise and excitement to subside, then he gestured for them all to sit down. "This card arrived yesterday, and I couldn't believe what I was seeing when I opened it. Maddie's been living in Ireland these past eight years, and she's got two kids. I'm a grandad," he beamed, as he passed a photo to Debbie and the others moved to her desk to look at it. Slater returned the photo to Bentley, and they all sat down again. "I've been on the blower to the CC, and he's delighted for me as well. Maddie says in her letter that she, her partner and my grandchildren," he paused, beaming again, "are coming to Scarborough to meet us sometime next year. So, my friends, the other bit of good news is that we can close that Missing Person file!" Sharpe cheered, and the others applauded enthusiastically.

"At last we can close the curtain on that Dixon nightmare from the summer," Debbie Chapman added. [1]

"Exactly," Bentley continued, "we've had a lousy few months digging up bodies, searching for a serial killer, dealing with juvenile arsonists, and almost losing one of our own … so finally, a bit of good news." He paused, glancing at Debbie, then adding: "How is Fiona, by the way?"

"She's good, Sir, getting there I think." Ryan looked out of the window.

"I'm pleased to hear it," Bentley smiled at the DS. "One last thing. Jean and I are going to have a bit of a party at our house on Saturday night. There'll be plenty of booze to drink and bites to eat, so I hope you can all call in at some point in the evening. Bring your partners, or," glancing at Ryan, "a friend, if you want." A few enthusiastic nods. "Right, down to business," he said, rummaging in his pocket for a jelly-baby and finding a red one, which he popped into his mouth. "George … your serial shoplifter. Where are we with this bloody nuisance?"

1 See 'The Golden Chrysanthemums'

CHAPTER FOUR

George Ryan thought about the evening ahead as he showered unenthusiastically. He couldn't help feeling that he would be the odd one out, with everyone else showing up with a partner, but the news about Maddie had boosted the team and had saved the DI from early retirement, so Ryan felt it was his duty to go to Bentley's party. *I'll just show my face for half an hour, then make some excuse to leave, come home and watch "Match of the Day" on the telly,* he thought to himself. He managed a brief smile, dried off quickly, and headed into the bedroom to get ready. *Something casual.* He fished out a clean pair of jeans and a green polo shirt from the wardrobe, dressed quickly, and looked out of the window to check the weather. Raining again. Five days to go, and no chance of a White Christmas. He decided to drive to Bentley's house, then he had an excuse not to drink too much and could leave early if he wanted to. Earlier that day he had heard Debbie Chapman telling Bentley that Fiona Charlton was spending Christmas with her family in Liverpool, so there was a good chance that she would not be at the party. Ryan wanted to see her again, wanted to ask her a whole list of questions, but it would be a lot easier if she was already on her way home.

Ryan checked around the flat, locked up and headed out to his car, making a mental note to buy a bottle of wine on the way.

***

The road was choked with cars by the time Ryan arrived at Bentley's house, a decent-sized semi on Scarborough's North Bay, so he parked his car in a neighbouring street and walked back. Bentley's wife Jean greeted him at the door and ushered him through to the kitchen, where a good range of beers and wines was scattered on the worktop. Ryan deposited his bottle of Pinot, opened a bottle of Speckled Hen, and headed for the back lounge, where a table was groaning with buffet food. He took a swig of his beer, glanced around the room and went over to chat to Dennis Slater, who was also on his own. Bentley was engaged in a lively conversation with a family friend. Tim Sharpe arrived, to everyone's surprise, and pushed through to find a seat for his partner Laura, an attractive young woman with long, dark hair, and heavily pregnant. He introduced her to the others: "I think she's swallowed a basketball!" The small talk and occasional laughter drifted on.

Debbie and Fiona arrived about thirty minutes after Ryan, and they joined the group of colleagues in the lounge. George Ryan cast an embarrassed glance at Fiona, smiled briefly as she turned and, to his surprise, she smiled back widely. Ryan chatted to the others, casting an occasional glance in Fiona's direction, then he filled a plate with sandwiches and sausage rolls and moved around the group. Fiona was the last to be offered a snack, and she mouthed *Thanks*, took a ham sandwich and smiled again. Debbie refused and whispered in Ryan's ear: "I'm leaving in a few minutes, George. Look after Fiona, won't you?" Ryan nodded and moved away from the group, trying to fathom out what was going on. He went back into the kitchen and poured another Speckled Hen.

Debbie Chapman was saying her goodbyes to Don and Jean Bentley, and she looked back and waved to Ryan as she left the room. Sharpe brushed past Ryan as he made for the kitchen and winked, gesturing his thumb at Fiona behind him. *He doesn't miss a trick,* Ryan thought, as he shuffled back into the lounge. One of the Whitby team was talking to Fiona, and it was over five minutes before she was alone again. Ryan gulped some of his beer, smiled across the room at Fiona, and moved over to her side. "Hi," he muttered, "long time no see … how are you?

"I'm good, George," she replied, smiling again, "are you OK?"

"Yes," he muttered, nodding, then glancing around the room, trying to avoid catching Sharpe's eye. He turned back to Fiona, as she adjusted her blonde hair over her shoulders. "Sorry," he continued meekly, "but meeting again like this, I feel a bit embarrassed, Fi."

"Don't, George, there's no need, honestly," she smiled, touching his arm. "Why don't you drink up, and we'll head into town?" Ryan looked puzzled.

"OK, but only if you're sure?" She nodded. "Alright, but let's say a few goodbyes before we go." They moved around, speaking briefly to their colleagues, before chatting to the Bentleys together, then leaving. George put his arm around Fiona, and then he guided her to the gate. "I'm parked around the corner … not too far away. I'll go and park near my flat, then we can walk into town. Is that OK?"

"Yes, whatever, George," she laughed and gripped his arm. "Let's go and enjoy ourselves, then afterwards … well, there are things I need to say, things I have to tell you, George." He looked puzzled again. "Come on," she giggled, pushing him along the pavement.

***

Two hours later, in the Merchant Irish Bar, George watched as Fiona headed for the loo, and tried to understand what was going on. He couldn't help feeling that this was a dream. He was a little worse for wear, but since leaving the Bentley's he and Fiona had chatted and laughed almost non-stop, just as they had in the summer, before she had been snatched by the serial killer Gregory Dixon, then afterwards had moved in with Debbie Chapman. Their conversation had been lively, but not serious, and Fiona had not mentioned "the things she needed to say", or if she had, George had let them pass him by. He stood up as she returned, and they put on their jackets and moved to the doorway. "I'll look for a taxi, shall I?"

"We can walk to your place, George, that is if you're still able to walk in a straight line," she added, laughing. "Come on," she instructed, linking arms and pushing past a group of young women who were trying to get into the pub. They walked briskly, passing a Chinese takeaway in a nearby street.

"Do you …?" George began to ask.

"Keep moving," she grinned, "you and your belly." Ten minutes later, they were outside George's flat. He ushered her into the lounge and switched on a table-lamp, then nipped into the hall to hang up their jackets. Fiona, her long blonde hair tumbling down her shoulder, was standing near the sofa when he returned, so he gestured for her to sit down.

"What would you like to drink, Fi," he asked, "I've got …?"

"Forget the drink, and the talking, George," she smiled, kissing him lightly on the cheek and taking hold of his hand, "we've got some unfinished business, I think."

"What …" George began, looking absolutely baffled.

"Stop gawping, DC Ryan, let's see what you've got," she laughed, as she guided him towards the bedroom and opened the door. She pushed him inside and onto the bed, then kicked the door shut.

***

George stirred and rolled slowly onto his side, shaking an arm on which he had been lying. He lay still for a few more seconds, then opened his eyes slowly, blinking at a narrow shaft of sunlight from the curtains, then he tried to gather his thoughts. Where am I? He twisted around to glance at the other side of the bed, where the sheets had been thrown back, but no one was there. Fiona? Was last night a dream? He sat up quickly and swung his legs over the edge of the bed, then tried to stand up. His back and legs were aching, and he swayed slightly. George rubbed his eyes, pulled on a pair of shorts, opened the door and followed an aroma of coffee to the kitchen.

"Hello, Sleepyhead," Fiona smiled as he eased open the door. She was wearing his green dressing-gown, her blonde hair tumbling loosely down her back, and was bare-footed. "Good timing, young man! The coffee's ready, and I've made some bacon sandwiches. I couldn't find much else in the fridge!" George rubbed his eyes again.

"Morning … I think." He glanced at the sandwiches. "Sorry there isn't more, but I don't do much entertaining." He smiled briefly, then reached for the table. "That was some night," he said, grinning. "I'm aching all over."

"Lightweight," she laughed, lifting the plate of sandwiches. "Come on, let's have a drink and eat these." She headed for the lounge, as George picked up the coffees and followed her.

***

Later that morning, they showered, then made love again, this time more gently, less frantic that the previous night. Afterwards, George sat up against the pillows, cradling Fiona in his arms, relaxing now, and casting his mind back to the party at Bentley's house.

Silence, apart from their breathing.

"Last night, Fi, at the DI's house," George spoke quietly, "you told me that you had things to say, to tell me, I think. I'd like to hear them, because last night was great, really great, but I'm struggling to make sense of it all … you know, when we got on great during the summer, then you had that horrific ordeal at Dixon's hands, and afterwards moved in with Debbie," he paused, "then last night. It's all been a bit surreal, Fiona, and I can't get my head round it." Fiona eased herself up, and arranged some pillows behind her back, strands of her long blonde hair clinging to her breasts.

"I've wanted to talk to you for a long time, George, but it's been difficult finding the right moment … but after last night you're due an explanation. Look, let's get dressed and have another coffee, then I can tell you everything. OK?" He nodded, and they searched for their clothes.

***

"Do you remember, not long after we first dated, that you asked me about previous boyfriends?"

"Yes, I do," George replied, sipping his coffee, "and I remember that you told me that you'd had some *shitty* relationships, I think that was how you described them."

"Probably, but there was one relationship in particular." Fiona thought for a minute or two, as George waited patiently, sipping his coffee again. "About seven years ago, when I was eighteen or nineteen, I was working part-time in a bar in Liverpool, and one evening Gary Henderson came in and ordered a drink. I didn't know him, but I honestly went weak at the knees," she continued, blushing. "He was really good-looking, George, absolutely gorgeous. He was blond-haired, like me, had a cheeky face, and the most beautiful deep-blue eyes I've ever seen. I'm sorry, George, but I just melted, I was literally shaking as I served him." She paused, glancing away, and George placed his coffee mug on the floor, then smiled at her.

"It's OK, Fiona, when you're ready," he spoke quietly, touching her arm.

"He took me home that night, and before too long I had moved in with him. He was a real charmer, George, and he treated me very well, you know, took me out for nice meals, bought expensive clothes for me. My family loved him, he was so polite, well-mannered, and as I've said before, really charming. My life was put on hold," she continued, glancing at George. "I had thought of going to university, but

I really fancied joining the police and had enough qualifications to do that once I was twenty-one."

"What did he do for a living?"

"Well, that was the thing, I never knew, never asked. I just assumed he was a businessman of some sort. Sometimes he was out late, sometimes away for a few days, but I never asked questions, as I assumed that it was all part of his business life. He was never short of money, always had a nice car, nice clothes." George nodded. "I wasn't locked up or anything," she said, laughing, "I was free to meet my friends, even to spend a weekend away with them if I wanted to. Gary never asked questions as well."

"How old was he?"

"I can't remember exactly, but about ten years older than me. He looked so young, with his cheeky grin." She glanced at George, then took his hand. "Things like age, work, etc didn't seem to be important, George. I was so happy … I was in love with him."

"So what happened, Fiona, what went wrong? He sounds the perfect partner."

"Drugs, George. My best friend in Liverpool died from a drug overdose, then a couple of my other friends told me that they had heard whispers about Gary. I couldn't believe them at first, and just ignored them, until one night some of his business contacts met at his house. I was getting ready to go out with some friends, but I'd slipped downstairs for my handbag and overheard some of their conversation when I was in the back room." She stood up and moved to the window, before continuing. "Gary didn't do drugs, and he wasn't a street dealer. He was much bigger than that, George, and I overheard them discussing a big deal that evening. Two nights later, it was on the news that the police had missed a big drugs haul in the city. I didn't do anything at the time, but a couple of months later, Gary told me that was inviting some of his friends around for a card session. I left as one or two of them were arriving, and I'd planted a listening device in the lounge. A couple of days later, when I was on my own, I retrieved the device and took it to the police. They showed me photographs of known drug dealers in the area, and I was able to identify some of them. The information I provided helped the police capture most of the gang when the next big haul was due." Fiona put her head in her hands. "I betrayed Gary. I loved him, George, but I grassed on him and helped to send him to prison."

"Were any serious threats made against you before or after the trial?"

"Not by Gary or any of the others who were convicted, though I had a few nasty brushes with members of their families. His mother, Janet I think she was called, was a real nasty piece of work, and horrible to me outside the courthouse. Criminals in Liverpool have a code of honour, George. They don't like grasses."

"I guess it was soon after the trial that you decided to join the police, and to move away from the area?"

"Pretty much, yes. I moved away to live with some relatives in Surrey, but I didn't like it down there, so eventually I began to think about a career in the police. North Yorkshire sounded a nice place to be, so I sent in my application, did my training, and here I am!"

"That's quite a story, Fiona, another frightening time for you. You've certainly been through the wars!" He smiled briefly, then looked thoughtful. "You still haven't told me why you moved in with Debbie, Fi?"

"As I told you before, there haven't been any threats made against me since the trial, but criminals have long memories, George. At the back of my mind there's always been this nagging question: What will happen when Gary is released? I don't know the answer to that. Part of me says that nothing will happen, as any action against me would put him behind bars for a long time, but you never know, do you?" George waited for her to continue. "That's why I decided not to get involved with another bloke until some time after Gary is released, until I was sure that any future relationship I have would be safe. That was my plan until you came along, George!" She laughed, and George smiled, waiting again for her to complete the story. "I know that you were on the verge of asking me to move in with you, but as I have said before, I didn't want to commit myself to you until Gary is well out of the way. Then I was attacked by that nutter Dixon last September, and I felt very vulnerable. I was worried about being alone. That's why I had a word with Debbie about sharing her house, then moved in with her. I thought that no-one would attack me if I was living with a policewoman."

"Right, so are you saying …?"

"That I'm not a lesbian, or bi-sexual?" she smiled, shaking her head. "You should know the answer to that question, especially after last night! Well, I am not, George, but as for Debbie, well, I don't know, as she keeps her private life to herself. She has a close friend who lives near Leeds, where she came from, but I've never asked. She went there after Bentley's party. I discussed everything with Debbie, and she agreed to go along with it. We thought that if that arsehole Sharpe spread it around that we were lesbians, well, that would be more protection for me. Do you understand?"

"I think so," George smiled briefly. "Let me get this right. There might be a future for us, Fiona, but only after Gary Henderson is released? You have to be sure that he's not looking for revenge, is that it?" She nodded slowly. "OK, then I can wait too. When is he due to be released?

"His parole hearing is next month."

***

Fiona stayed with George until late afternoon, then prepared to return to Debbie's house. She declined a lift, but they both kissed passionately on the doorstep before Fiona walked along the street, before turning back and waving to George. The thin man sitting in the red Astra parked across the street removed his glasses, wrote something in a notepad, waited until George had closed the door, then put his glasses back on and started the engine.

CHAPTER FIVE

Tim Sharpe was waiting to pounce on George Ryan as soon as he arrived for the Monday morning briefing. Bentley and Debbie were still out of the Incident Room, so Sharpe took his chance. "My, my, young George, you're a real dark horse. Sneaking off with the delicious Fiona, when everybody thought she was out of bounds?" He glanced towards the door, as Debbie entered the room. "The plot thickens," he muttered, grinning. "I'll have words with you later, my son."

"Don't bother, Tim. It's got nothing to do with you." Ryan turned away as Debbie moved to her desk and sat down. She looked across at Ryan, and smiled, then Bentley appeared in the doorway.

"'Morning, everybody," Bentley said briskly, "I hope you all had a nice weekend. Thanks for showing your faces on Saturday evening, folks … Jean and I both appreciated your company." He smiled. "It was a good evening. I hope we haven't got too many sore heads today!" He glanced at a few papers before continuing. "We don't seem to have much on at the moment, which is great as Christmas is just around the corner. Is there anything I need to know about?" he asked, delving into his pocket for a jelly-baby.

"Just one thing, Gov," Sharpe replied, "we just received a report about a domestic in the Old Town. The hospital phoned about five minutes ago. They told us that they have some bloke with serious head wounds in the A & E."

"Did they mention who caused the wounds?" Debbie asked.

"Yeah … his missus," Sharpe laughed softly.

"OK, Sharpie, I bet he's not laughing," Bentley muttered solemnly. "Nip to the hospital and get some details. Are you busy, George?"

"I'm still dealing with that shoplifter, Sir."

"Oh, yes … Debbie?" he turned to her.

"Alright, Sir, I'll hold his hand. Do you want some body armour, Sharpie?" she smirked, standing up then heading for the door. Sharpe grabbed his coat, and followed her.

"No need, Debbie, you're the expert at dealing with women." He grinned at Ryan, then put on a serious face as Debbie gave him a filthy look.

***

Chris Woodend glanced nervously at the other people who were queueing to visit some of the inmates at Strangeways Gaol in Manchester. He tugged at one of his prominent ears, then pushed it back under his hair. He was a thin, wiry figure, which made his ears look even bigger. One of his classmates had christened him "Wingnut", and the name had stuck ever since. There was a brief silence as one of the warders opened the doors to the visiting room, then the queue surged forward. Woodend looked around the room, then caught sight of Gary Henderson, who was sitting at a corner table. He smiled, then threaded his way through the other tables and sat down opposite Henderson.

"Hiya, Gary, how's things?"

"Just the same as last week, Chris, and last month, and last year. Nothing changes in here," he smiled briefly. "You should know."

"Yeah, but it was a long time ago, Gary. I've tried to forget about that time." He looked into Henderson's blue eyes, then glanced down before continuing. "Is everything still OK for your parole hearing?"

"I think so, my friend. My solicitor is quite confident that I'll be out of here soon. He'd better be right on that one. I'm paying him plenty."

"He's right, Gary, isn't he, because you've kept your nose clean in here, haven't you?"

"I've been whiter than white, Wingnut, purer than the driven snow. Since I've been rotting in here, I've been Charm personified, never said Boo! to a goose …" he paused, smiling broadly at the diminutive figure across the table. "It's all been Yes, Sir, No, Sir, Three Bags Full, Sir and in a few days, Chris, I'm going to put all of that a good distance behind me. But before I do, there is one matter that I have to settle, isn't there?" He opened his eyes widely, and fixed them on Woodend. "You've had a nice little holiday in Scarborough, Chris. Tell me about Fiona Charlton."

"She's still working at Whitby, and she's still living at that policewoman's house in Scarborough."

"Chapman … I think that's her name?"

"Yeah, that's right."

"She's been there a few months, hasn't she? Have you ever seen them out together?"

"No, I haven't."

"I can't weigh this one up, Chris. We had a great relationship, and she liked sex … plenty of it … so why hasn't she been out with another bloke? There's been nothing for all these years that I've been stuck in here, at least as far as I know," he continued thoughtfully. "I can understand if she's being secretive about a new relationship, but one with a woman? I can't help thinking that she's still in love with me, even if she did grass on me all those years ago. It's confusing, Chris, and I can't get my head around it all." He paused, staring at his gopher across the table. "All I know is that I need to see her after I get out of here, and find out if she still wants to be with me." He smiled. "I'm a forgiving sort of a bloke underneath, Chris, and I can understand that she was really upset when her best mate overdosed."

"Yeah," Woodend muttered quietly, "I think I'd better tell you, Gary, that she did see a bloke last weekend. She went with that policewoman,

Chapman, to a party in town, then the policewoman left, and soon afterwards Fiona left … with a young man. I followed them to his house or flat, and Fiona stayed all night. I saw her leave on Sunday afternoon." Henderson's gaze hardened.

"So there might be a secret relationship after all, another bloke that she's kept hidden under the bushes." He grimaced.

"They kissed pretty passionately before she left," Woodend muttered, shrinking back in his seat.

"In that case, Wingnut, you'd better get your skinny arse back to Scarborough and do some more digging for me. If you do unearth a secret boyfriend, I want his balls on a plate!"

CHAPTER SIX

Christmas 1997 came and went, and things settled down for the CID team at Northway in Scarborough. The shoplifter was cautioned … again, and the domestic in the Old Town proved to be less serious than Bentley had first thought … just another couple with too much time together at home at Christmas, and too much alcohol. The man was discharged from hospital a day later, and he refused to press any charges against his partner, telling Chapman and Sharpe that it was "just a misunderstanding."

"Arsehole," muttered Sharpe, as he and Chapman left the hospital. "You watch, he'll be back in there after New Year. Now that she's got away with it, she's bound to assault him again."

"You're probably right, Sharpie, but not everyone's got your charming personality. I bet half the couples in Scarborough, or anywhere else come to think of it, have occasional rows like that. It's just that there's rarely a knife handy."

"Maybe, but nothing like that is going to happen

in my house," Sharpe replied philosophically, as they reached the car.

"That's what you think, pal. Just wait until Laura realises that you've forgotten to change a nappie!"

***

The team scattered for a few days over Christmas: Debbie Chapman to somewhere in Leeds; Dennis Slater and his wife travelled to Leigh, near Wigan, to spend Christmas with their son, his wife Katie, their two-year-old daughter and Katie's family, who lived nearby; Tim Sharpe managed to behave himself for a few hours at Laura's parents on the north side of Scarborough, where her family eagerly anticipated the birth of a new grandchild; and a similar air of anticipation hung around in the Bentley household, where the DI and his wife Jean half-expected to find another letter from Maggie on the doormat every time they left the house, or to hear her voice whenever the phone rang. Bentley remained on standby over the Christmas break, generously, and unusually for him, giving the rest of the team some time off.

Fiona Charlton and George Ryan met for a coffee in a café on Eastborough before returning to their families for a Christmas break – Fiona to Aintree, near Liverpool, and George to Darlington. They exchanged gifts before Fiona made her way to the train station, and George drove the sixty miles or so to his parents' house. Though back in Liverpool, her reunion with George had made Fiona stronger, and less pessimistic about the future; for George, even the predictability of a traditional family Christmas seemed more appealing this year.

***

Phoebe Bartlett enjoyed entertaining at Christmas and New Year, even if it meant spending a lot of time with her husband's relatives and friends whom she disliked. She had taken several days to decorate the house, inviting the neighbouring Archer children to lend a hand. They had visited again on Christmas morning, as Phoebe loved buying the gifts for them that one time she longed would have been for her own children. The distractions of the festive celebrations, however, were overshadowed this year by her feelings for Jack Mason. She regretted her decision not to see him until after the New Year, but now it was too late … and too risky to attempt to contact him. *January will soon be here*, she reminded herself more than once, and tried to concentrate on the arrangements for the New Year's party which she had arranged ever since her marriage to Arthur Bartlett. The guest-list varied from year to year, but it always included the Bartletts' near neighbours, her sister Melissa, and Arthur's closest relatives and friends. It was primarily an adult affair, with only the Archer children in attendance, but Phoebe made sure that they really enjoyed themselves. She organised a few party games and quizzes, made sure that Robin and Amelia had some video games to play on their own … then there was the firework display at midnight. Phoebe spent considerable time and expense to organise a display that was bigger and better than the previous year. Many people living in that area of Filey looked forward to "Phoebe's Fireworks", as the annual display became popularly known. Once the distraction of the children and the neighbours had gone, Phoebe could at last turn to generous measures of alcohol to deaden the necessity of spending some time with her relatives. *After a few glasses, I won't give a toss!* she consoled herself before the big day.

***

The evening had gone well ... far better that Phoebe could have imagined. The atmosphere was friendlier than before, and everyone seemed to get on so well with each other. Tom Galbraith had invited two of his crew to assist with the fireworks display, and they added a lively element to the proceedings. The food had largely disappeared, the games were over, and now it was time for the fireworks display. Despite the wintry chill, everyone found thick coats to wear and gathered outside on the extensive lawns at the back of the house. The countdown to the New Year was chanted loudly, then cheers accompanied the first fireworks. Phoebe liked her displays to be spectacular, colourful and memorable, rather than just a loud noise. For the next twenty minutes, the skies above the Bartletts' house dazzled those watching then, suddenly, it was all over and everyone made a dash to find the warmth of the house. The buzz of the excitement was followed by a chorus of thanks and farewells, with Phoebe and Arthur in centre stage, then many of the guests searched for their belongings and gifts and headed for the front door, walking back to their houses on the estate or driving away into the darkness. Phoebe hugged the tiny figure of Amelia, then the Archers headed for the gateway, leaving just a handful of guests at Mandalay.

"That was a great party, Phoebe," Melissa gushed, as her sister made her way to the kitchen.

"Yes, it was good, sis, but now that the fireworks are over and most people have gone, I can finally relax." She glanced around, looking for her husband. "I need a drink," she smiled.

"Prosecco?"

"Of course, open the bottle, dear, and pour me a glass. I'm gasping." The remaining guests clustered around, as a cork was popped, drinks were poured and a murmur of conversation began.

"There are glasses of prosecco on the tray," someone muttered, as one of them was handed to Phoebe.

"God, that didn't touch the sides," she drained the glass, turned slightly and nudged Harold Hardy, her husband's best friend. "Be a darling, Wee Willie Winkie," she whispered, "and pass me another." She glanced around the room, then took a sip as the glass was handed to her. "Happy New Year everyone!"

Another cork was popped, another bottle opened … more drinks, more toasts, more conversation … Phoebe reached for another glass.

• PART TWO •

CHAPTER SEVEN

"I want to report a missing person." The desk sergeant looked up at the dark-haired young man standing in front of him, and paused. "A missing person," the young man repeated anxiously and nodded.

"OK, Sir, a missing person then," he muttered, reaching for a form in a nearby cabinet. "This missing person, Sir … do we have a name?"

"Yes … Phoebe."

"Phoebe what?"

"I don't know. I just know that her first name is Phoebe."

"I see." He wrote on the form, then looked up. "Address?"

"I don't know," the man shrugged. "I'm sorry, but I don't know many details. I only know her name, her phone number, and I can give you a description." The sergeant raised his eyebrows, waiting for more information, his pen poised. "Look, sergeant," the young man continued, relaxing a little, "I've been seeing Phoebe for about two months, but since New Year I've not been able to contact her." He grimaced. "She's gone missing." The sergeant scratched his head.

"And your name is …?"

"Jack Mason."

"OK, Mr Mason, take a seat over there," he gestured, "and I'll get someone down to have a word with you." He waited until Mason had sat down on the other side of the room, then he turned to his phone, lifted it and spoke softly. "Sharpie, I've got a young bloke down here, and it looks as if he's lost his girlfriend. Can you pop down and have a few words?" A pause. "Jack Mason." Another pause. "Cheers." He glanced across the room. "One of the CID team will be down in a few minutes, Mr Mason. OK?"

***

"Would you like a drink before we start, Mr Mason?"

"No thanks, I'm fine … and please call me Jack."

"OK, Jack," Tim Sharpe replied, easing back in his chair. "You're Jack Mason, the footballer, aren't you?" The young man smiled. "I sometimes get down to the Athletic Ground. My mates and I always stand in the "Cow Shed", he added. "I've seen you play a few times. You're good." Another smile. "Right, down to business. You've come in to report a missing person, is that right?" Mason nodded. "OK, let's get some details," he said, opening his notepad.

"It's my girlfriend, or at least a woman I've been

seeing for about two months. She's called Phoebe."

"Phoebe what?"

"I don't know. As I told the sergeant, I can't give you many details. We met at a club function in mid-November, and I saw her a few times in December. She's blond-haired, good-looking, and probably in her early thirties. This is her phone number," he continued, passing over a piece of paper.

"Anything else, Jack?"

"Naw, that's it." Sharpe glanced out of the window. "Look, I know what you're thinking, but Phoebe and I got on great. I've had plenty of women, but Phoebe is a stunner and I know she really fancies me. She told me that we wouldn't be able to see each other over Christmas and New Year … too many family things," he paused, "but she told me to phone her in January and we'd continue where we left off." He gripped the table and leant forward. "I'm not messing you about, Detective, something's happened to her."

***

"What's amusing you?" Debbie Chapman asked as Sharpe, grinning, returned to the Incident Room. Sharpe glanced towards the door, as DI Bentley appeared.

"I've just interviewed the Seadogs' star striker, and he's a bit upset because his girlfriend has dumped him," he replied, pouting.

"OK, Tim," Bentley muttered gruffly, "cut the bullshit and tell us what's happened."

"Well, Sir, that's pretty much the truth. We've just had Jack Mason in here," he replied, pausing as Bentley looked blank, "he's Scarborough FC's leading scorer, Sir, and it looks to me if he's been screwing some married woman, until she saw sense over Christmas. He hasn't seen her for a few weeks, and he wants to report her missing."

"What's she called, Tim?" Ryan asked.

"That's the joke, George. He said she's called Phoebe," he continued, laughing, "as if any woman is called Phoebe these days. Like I said, she's probably married, and she's had a bit of fun with him, given him a false name and phone number, then dumped him."

"No surname, Sharpie?" Debbie asked.

"No, that's it … just Phoebe, a landline number, and a brief description. He told me that she's a stunning blonde in her early thirties." He glanced around the room. "That's all, folks." He added, in a Bugs Bunny voice.

"Right, cut out the comedy act," Bentley barked, glaring at Sharpe. "Have you tried the landline number yet?"

"No, Sir, I've just come up from the interview."

"Well, you'd better …"

"Sir," the quiet Dennis Slater interrupted, "before you make that call," he continued, stroking his chin, "I know of a local woman called Phoebe who fits that description."

"Really, Dennis, tell us more."

"As I said, I know of a woman called Phoebe. She's a second cousin, or something like that, of my wife. I've seen her at a couple of family dos, but I haven't spoken to her. She is a blonde, and very good-looking, Sir, so it could be her. Shall I …?"

"Yes, Dennis," Bentley continued, frowning as he searched for a jelly-baby in his pocket, "give the missus a ring."

***

Later in the afternoon, Bentley stopped writing on the whiteboard, and turned to speak to the others. "This is what we've been able to add to Jack Mason's information," he spoke, looking directly at Sharpe. "Dennis' wife has given us some more details, and we've checked them out." He pointed to the whiteboard. "Phoebe Bartlett, blonde, early forties, married to Arthur Bartlett, a local jeweller."

"That big shop here on Eastborough, Sir?" Debbie asked.

"Yes, as well as shops in Bridlington and Filey. He's in his mid-fifties, and he and Phoebe live in a large house on the outskirts of Filey. The landline checks out … it's their home phone number."

"Jack Mason said that he was only allowed to use that number during the day," Sharpe added.

"That makes sense," Debbie continued. "She only wanted him to contact her when her husband was at one of his shops." Bentley nodded.

"Dennis' wife also told us that there was a photo in the local rag showing Phoebe getting into Mason's car."

"When was that?" Ryan asked.

"Early December, she thinks, a few weeks before Christmas," Slater replied. "Phoebe wasn't named … they just called her a mystery blonde … but Jack Mason was. I'll get a copy of the photo from the Scarborough Evening News."

"I tried the Bartlett's number about twenty minutes ago," Bentley informed the group, "but there was no reply. I'll try again in half an hour, but if I draw a blank … well, we need to pay them a visit. Debbie, I think you'll be more diplomatic than these other jokers," he glanced at the men, "so I want you to pay the Bartletts a visit this evening and see if we do have a missing person. Take George with you, but you do all of the talking. Don't mention Jack Mason. OK?"

"Alright, Boss, but Dennis has done most of the legwork, so …"

"No, Debbie, with his wife's connection, Dennis is too close, and as for Tim, too risky."

"Cheers, Sir," Sharpe muttered.

"If she is there, Tim, I don't want you drooling over her. George is the safer option."

"Yeah," Sharpe muttered under his breath, turning to look at Ryan, "no danger there."

"You've got that footballer's number, haven't you, Tim?" Bentley asked. Sharpe nodded. "OK, then you and Dennis can check out the phone records. Find out when he phoned the Bartletts' house. Oh, and see if any of them has a mobile, and check those out as well. Let's find out exactly who's been phoning who." He stood up and turned to go to his office. "Debbie, George, a quick word please." They both followed him, and Ryan smiled when he saw the newly-framed photograph of Bentley's daughter and her family in pride of place on his desk. "Sit down, please." A pause. "Debbie, when you go to Filey tonight, if Phoebe Bartlett is there with her husband, then just make your excuses quickly and tell them that there's been a misunderstanding. If you can get her on her own, then quickly fill her in on the details and ask her to contact this Mason bloke." He paused. "On the other hand, if there's no sign of her, you'll have to tread lightly, Debbie. I want you to note Arthur Bartlett's reaction when you tell him that someone has reported his wife as being missing. Be vague, don't mention the source, right? We need to find out what kind of relationship they have … you know what I mean?"

"Yes, of course, Sir, but somehow I don't think he'll be surprised. I doubt if this fling with Jack Mason is the first one she's had."

"Maybe." He turned to look at Ryan. "As I said before, George, let Debbie do the talking, but I want you to have a good look around when you're at the house. Check out the cars, see if there are any security cameras, note which photos are on display, look for any signs that Phoebe's been there recently … that sort of thing." He laughed softly. "Look, this will probably turn out to be a waste of time, but if Phoebe isn't there, bloody-well make sure that Mr

Bartlett tells you exactly where she's supposed to be. I don't want us chasing our tails on this one, OK?"

***

Debbie Chapman called at Ryan's house just after 6pm, and they headed along the A165, following the coast. "Everything OK, George?" she asked, glancing at him.

"Yeah, fine, thanks Debbie." He peered out of the window. "I haven't been to Filey before."

"It used to be really busy, when the Butlin's camp was there," Chapman replied, "But after it closed Filey became a sleepy resort again."

"Right." A moment of silence. "I've been wondering … wondering what Fiona's told you."

"After Bentley's party?" Ryan nodded, and she smiled. "Well, George, she didn't go into details, but I gathered that you made up for lost time, and that she put you in the picture about her ex-boyfriend?"

"Yes, that was a bit of an eye-opener. She's terrified of him."

"Not quite, George, but she's certainly worried about what he might do if he gets parole from Strangeways. I've made some discreet enquiries, and it looks as if he's got a good chance of being released on parole. There'll be conditions attached to any release, of course, but Fiona seems to think that Henderson won't take too much notice of them. He's had a few years to consider what kind of revenge he may take on her."

"Do you really think he's that much of a threat?"

"Could be, George. Scum like him don't like grasses, and he doesn't sound like the forgiving kind."

"Surely he's got too much to lose, Debbie?"

"Maybe, but if he managed to salt away a lot of money before he was banged up, and if he still has people loyal to him, well … he is a danger."

"Does Bentley know about this?"

"Not yet, but we perhaps need to have a word with him before Henderson's hearing."

"Yes, definitely."

"And a word of advice for you, George. I know that you and Fiona have been very discreet in the past few weeks, but make sure that you're not seen openly as a couple. Let's see how things develop in the next couple of months before you start making wedding plans, OK?" They both laughed. "No, seriously, George, you need to keep your head below the parapet for a while. Don't start thinking that you're Sir Galahad. Gangsters like Henderson don't read Knights of the Round Table."

"Thanks for the advice, Debbie, but I don't want to see Fiona coming to any harm, especially after that episode with Dixon last year. Let's speak to Bentley tomorrow, OK?"

"Perhaps, but we'll make a decision after we've been to the Bartletts."

"Agreed." Ryan peered through a side window. "This is a bit of a weird one, Debbie," Ryan muttered, as the dark-haired DS drove along the Scarborough

Road, searching for the small exclusive estate on the outskirts of Filey where the Bartletts lived. "I think that footballer's been led a merry dance by Phoebe Bartlett, and we're going to look like a pair of clowns when we get there."

"Don't feel bad or embarrassed, George, just keep focused," she replied, glancing at him, then peering back along the road. "I hope this Phoebe woman is there, then we can really drop her in the shit and expose the double life she's been leading."

"Hmm, but as you told the Boss, Arthur Bartlett probably knows exactly what his wife is like." He again peered into the darkness outside the car. "I think we getting near, Debbie," then, as a sign loomed out of the gloom, "yes, this is it." The road ahead narrowed into a lane, but Chapman swung left, and the car's headlights illuminated a handful of large detached houses, two of them with security gates.

"What's the name of the house, George?"

"Mandalay."

"That's an odd name."

"Not really, Debbie. *Mandalay* was the ancient capital of Burma. I like the name … it sounds mysterious, I think."

"Well, let's hope that there's no big mystery here, George, then I can get back home and watch Coronation Street." George smiled to himself, then pointed.

"Over there, Debbie." The security gate was

closed, so Chapman parked the car and switched off the engine.

"Ready, George?" Without looking at the young DC, she slipped out of the car, walked to the gate and pressed the button on the intercom. There was no reply, so she pressed it again. A few seconds later, a crackly voice replied.

"Yes, who is it?"

"North Yorkshire Police, Mr Bartlett. I'm DS Chapman, and DC Ryan is with me. May we come in and speak to you?"

"I'll come out to the gate. Push your warrant cards through the letter-box." Chapman glanced back at Ryan.

"Wait until he appears, George." Ryan nodded, then turned as a young girl appeared at the entrance to the neighbouring house. She was wearing a thick pink anorak and a matching woolly hat. Ryan smiled briefly, then turned as Chapman touched his arm. "I can hear somebody approaching, George. Where's your card?" she asked, as she pushed hers through the letter-box. The gate slowly opened, revealing a tall elegant-looking man wearing a long coat.

"It's cold out here," he said, looking at each police officer in turn and handing back their cards. "Follow me, please." Ryan took his card and looked behind him, as the young girl was being ushered back into her house by her mother. A sketch-pad tumbled to the ground, and the girl picked it up and followed her mother back into the house. Ryan turned around and walked briskly to catch up with the others. He glanced around, noting a large green Mercedes saloon on the driveway near the double-garage and a twin security camera covering the entrance to the house and the garage area. Ryan then entered the house through a huge wooden doorway to a hall, where Mr Bartlett was hanging Chapman's coat on a wooden stand. He eased his coat off his back, hung it next to Chapman's and followed the others through to a large lounge, where a roaring fire dominated the room. A large oil painting of Phoebe Bartlett dominated one of the walls, and Ryan spotted a framed photo of the Bartletts on one of the side tables. "Please, take a seat," Mr Bartlett instructed, gesturing towards a comfortable sofa. He waited until they had sat down, then he sat down in a nearby armchair. "Now, what can I do for you?"

"We're sorry to interrupt your evening, Mr Bartlett, but we need to know if your wife is here with you tonight."

"No, she isn't", Bartlett replied softly, puffing his cheeks and looking down at the floor.

"So, is she just out with friends, or …?"

"She's gone away, DS Chapman, she left just after New Year. I don't know where she's gone this time."

"*This time*, Mr Bartlett, so she's been away before without telling you where's she's going?"

"Exactly," he said, looking directly at Chapman. "Look," he paused for a few seconds, "I'm sure that you're aware that there's a considerable age difference between my wife and I?" Chapman glanced at Ryan, and nodded. "She's fourteen years younger than me, and she enjoys a lively social life, shall we say? I suffer from a bad back these days and find travelling stressful, so we tend to lead separate social lives. She's often gone away for a few days, or even gone on holiday, without telling me where she's going. I don't ask questions," he added, smiling, "because I know that she will be back in her own time. I'm a realist, DS Chapman, so I don't try to keep Phoebe caged up." Chapman and Ryan smiled. "Can you tell me who has asked you to call here and to question me?"

"I'm sorry, Mr Bartlett, but that's confidential. I'll just say that a friend has been trying unsuccessfully to contact her for a week or two." Bartlett smiled briefly, as Ryan asked a question.

"You said that you know that she will be back in her own time, Mr Bartlett. How can you be sure?"

"Well, DC … I'm sorry, I have forgotten your name."

"Ryan, Sir."

"Ah, DC Ryan, you're so young that you probably haven't experienced anything like this," Bartlett continued, smiling widely this time and pointing at the oil painting on the wall. "My wife is a good-looking woman … perhaps not as young as she tries to look … and she no longer finds me attractive … or interesting, but she is not stupid, DC Ryan. I treat her well, she has plenty of money at her disposal, and she can more or less do as she wishes … as long as she does not jeopardise everything we have here." He raised his arms and swept them around the room. "As you can see, we have a beautiful home, so Phoebe would be foolish to risk everything on, let's say, a fleeting amusement. Do you understand what I mean?"

"Yes," Ryan muttered, "thank you for being so honest."

"Do you have any children, Mr Bartlett," Chapman asked, "or close family, for example, where your wife may have gone to stay?"

"Not really, I'm sorry to say, Phoebe cannot have children. We both have a sister, but my wife is not very close to either of them." He paused for a few seconds. "She's probably gone on holiday to somewhere hot, DS Chapman. I'm sure that she will be back soon."

"Let's hope so, Mr Bartlett. Will you please get in touch as soon as she returns, or if you hear from her?"

"Of course," Bartlett replied, getting to his feet and glancing at the two police officers. "Now, is that all …?"

"Just one last question, Mr Bartlett," Ryan stood up as well. "Does your wife have a car?"

"Yes, she does, DC Ryan. It's one of those new Minis, you know, the bigger ones?" Ryan nodded. "She was driving it when she left on the third of January."

"I noticed that you have a security camera, Mr

Bartlett. Could we have a quick look at the images for that day, please?"

"Of course," Bartlett replied, standing up and heading for the study. "Please follow me." He switched on the recording machine, and fast-reversed the tape until he reached the third of January. He slowed the tape until they could see the late-morning images on the screen. It was an overcast day, but a blonde woman could be seen loading luggage into the boot, then driving off in the Mini. "There's my wife," Bartlett turned to the others, smiling. "Would you like to see anything else, DC Ryan?"

"No, thank you, Mr Bartlett," Ryan muttered, "I think that's all for now."

Bartlett ushered them to the front door, handed them their coats, and watched as they left his house. "Goodnight," he said as they walked down the steps to the gravelled driveway, then he closed the door firmly.

"Well, he was a cool customer," Chapman muttered to Ryan, as they heard Bartlett locking the door behind them.

CHAPTER EIGHT

Bentley waited until Dennis Slater had sat down before ushering Debbie Chapman to the front desk. He grabbed a red jelly-baby from the paper bag on the desk, then stood to one side. "The floor's all yours, Debbie. Tell us what you and young Ryan found out last night." He smiled at the others. "Was Phoebe Bartlett wrapped in a dressing-gown watching the telly?"

"Far from it, Sir, there was no sign of her. Mr Bartlett told us that she went away just after New Year."

"Saturday the third of January, to be exact," Ryan added, "and she drove off in her Mini."

"Skirt or car?" Sharpe turned and whispered to Slater.

"You're so hilarious, Sharpe!" Chapman barked.

"Sorry, sarge."

"As George was saying, Mrs Bartlett left on January the third. Mr Bartlett showed us the images for that morning on his security camera." Bentley tweaked some skin on his cheek, and reached for another jelly-baby as Chapman continued with her summary. "Mr Bartlett's story was that he and his wife have a very open marriage. He's fourteen years older than her, has a bad back, and lets her have a free rein to have what kind of social life she wants. He reckons that she won't rock the boat too much, as they have a fabulous house and plenty of money. Too much to lose on the local footballer, Sharpie."

"Where has she gone?" Bentley asked.

"Bartlett doesn't know. According to him, she's often gone away for days or weeks without telling him where's she going or contacting him when she's away." Bentley looked surprised. "He seemed very calm about it all, didn't he, George? He didn't appear to be worried at all."

"That's right, Debbie. He told us that he is a realist, and appeared to be quite confident that she will show up soon."

"Is that everything, Debbie?" Bentley rummaged for another jelly-baby.

"Pretty much, Sir."

"OK. What can you tell us about the phone records, Dennis?"

"I've listed the landline activity for the past month, Sir, and have highlighted the calls made by Jack Mason. As he told us, his calls have not been answered since New Year. The other calls fall into two groups: family and friends, and general utility calls … British Gas, that kind of thing. I've highlighted the frequent personal calls and checked them out. Mrs Bartlett has a sister who lives at Osmotherley, and Mr Bartlett has sister who lives at Whitby. He spends a lot of time with a bloke called Hardy, who lives nearby in Filey." He paused, glancing at the sheets. "The details are all on the sheet," he added, as he passed copies of two stapled A4 sheets to the others.

"Mobile records, Dennis?"

"Nothing, Sir. She doesn't own one."

"Right, let's consider the options. Phoebe Bartlett's been away for almost two weeks … enough time for a nice holiday in the sun, I suppose … but it won't harm if we do some checking, just in case she doesn't turn up. Dennis, can you chase up the details of Mrs Bartlett's car, and when you've done that, ring all of the local travel agents? Find out if she has booked a holiday with one of them. If you draw a blank, then get the airport authorities to start checking passenger lists for the third and fourth of January. Concentrate on Manchester and Leeds & Bradford first, alright?" Slater mouthed OK. "One other thing, Dennis. Have another word with your wife, and see if she can find out anything else about any family members who've seen Mrs Bartlett recently. George, you can give Dennis a hand. The rest of us can have a word with these people who've phoned Mr Bartlett. Tim, Mrs Bartlett's sister lives at Osmotherley. Give her a ring and if she's at home, go and pay her a visit. Debbie, this bloke Harold Hardy … a friend of Mr Bartlett. He lives nearby in

Filey, so go and see what he has to say. Find out if there are any more friends that we need to interview, then give Dennis and George a hand when you get back. I'll see Bartlett's sister and her husband. They live near Whitby, so I'll be able to top up my stock of jelly-babies," he added, smiling. "We'll discuss our findings in the morning, then decide what to do next." He paused, thoughtful. "I've got a funny feeling about this one."

"Osmotherley, Christ!" Sharpe nudged Slater. "That's somewhere on the other side of the North York Moors, isn't it, Dennis?" Slater nodded, and smiled. "How do I bloody get to it?"

"It's a nice old mining village, Tim, and it's easy to get there. Just follow the A170 to Thirsk, then take the A19 north to Osmotherley."

"To Thirsk? Christ, I'll have to go down Sutton Bank, won't I?"

"Yes," Slater grinned, "enjoy the view, Tim!"

"The road could be icy as hell," Sharpe grimaced and turned to Ryan. "You're a lucky bugger, Ryan," Sharpe muttered as the others began to move around the room. "Helping Dennis in this nice warm room, while I have to flit across the Moors on these bloody icy roads."

"I don't know why you're moaning, Tim. If Mrs Bartlett's sister is another stunning …"

"She'll be the Ugly Sister, pal, I can guarantee it."

***

Sharpe pulled off the A19 and eased into a lay-by, flicked the gear into neutral and checked the details in his notepad. Melissa Jordan, he thought to himself, her parents must have liked Greek names … Melissa, Phoebe. Melissa was the older sister, fifty-one years old, unmarried. He made a mental note of the address, then followed the signs towards Osmotherley. The road was clear, but small banks of snow were piled up on the verges. As he drove towards the village centre, Sharpe noted three pubs in quick succession, and smiled to himself. Get the interview over and done with, then a quick pint before returning back to base. If he timed it right, there would be just enough time to call in at the station, then get home to his partner Laura, who was due to give birth at any time. Sharpe turned right at the market cross, and eased along North End, looking for Melissa Jordan's cottage in a row of sandstone buildings. He parked his car, looked for a clear path across the snowy verges, and rang the bell on Melissa Jordan's door. A few seconds later, the door was opened by a plump, dark-haired lady with a welcoming smile. I knew it! Sharpe forced a smile.

"Melissa Jordan?"

"Yes, and you are …?"

"DC Sharpe, from Scarborough Police," he replied, showing her his warrant card. "I'd like to have a word with you about your sister."

"Oh, then please come in, officer," she smiled. "It's freezing out there. Go and sit by the fire, and I'll make a nice pot of tea." Sharpe took off his jacket and hung it on a coathook in the hall, then walked through into a cosy lounge. He stood by the fire, warming his hands as he gazed around the room. Country-style suite, family photos posing on the mantle-piece and framed on the walls, blue-and-white china on a Welsh dresser, a full plate-rack running around three of the four walls – *just like Mam's house!* Sharpe smiled to himself and sank into an armchair close to the fire, glancing towards the door as he heard Melissa Jordan nearing the doorway. She entered the room carrying a tray laden with a pot of tea, a selection of her best china, and a large plateful of gingerbread. Beaming at Sharpe, she set the tray down on a coffee-table, then sat down on the sofa and began pouring. "Help yourself," she gushed, pointing at the gingerbread, "I always win first prize at the annual show." Sharpe laughed politely, then reached for a sticky wedge, took a bite and placed it on a plate, licking his fingers.

"You're right," he muttered through a mouthful of gingerbread, "it's good." He continued eating as she poured him a cup of tea. Melissa sipped her tea and waited until he had finished eating.

"You said something about my sister, officer …?"

"Sharpe," he continued, "DC Tim Sharpe. Please call me Tim."

"Alright, Tim," she smiled, "and I'm called Melissa." Sharpe nodded.

"Your sister Phoebe has been reported as missing, Melissa. We've interviewed her husband, your brother-in-law Arthur Bartlett, but he can't tell us where she's gone. He told us that she went away just after New Year, on the third of January. She was driving her Mini car when she left." He paused. "To be frank, Melissa, Mr Bartlett didn't seem too concerned that his wife had gone away without telling him where she was going."

"Did Arthur report her missing?"

"No, it was a friend of hers." Melissa smiled briefly, then nodded slowly. "Mr Bartlett showed some images from his security camera to two of our officers, images taken when his wife drove away from their house. We've been making some enquiries, and I've travelled here today to see if you can help us, Melissa." He finished off the chunk of gingerbread, then added: "Has your sister been in touch to say where she's gone?"

"No, she hasn't, Tim, but this isn't the first time that Phoebe has done something like this. She and Arthur have a very open marriage, and Phoebe does pretty much as she pleases. She's disappeared for a few weeks with "a friend" in the past, so I expect that she'll turn up again when she's got fed up of this one."

"You don't sound very close to her, Melissa, if you don't mind my saying."

"Don't worry about it, Tim," she replied, smiling and offering him another sticky chunk, "it's common knowledge that we're chalk and cheese."

"Can you fill in a few more details for me?" Sharpe

asked, taking out his notepad. Melissa shifted along on the sofa.

"We're from Barnsley originally. I'm nearly nine years older than Phoebe, so we weren't really close as we grew up, you know … I was starting senior school when she was little more than a baby, and I'd left home when she was a teenager. I was seeing a lad called Keith from Osmotherley and we planned to marry, but he was killed in a car accident so it never happened. I'd got on really well with his family, so after Keith's death I decided to move up here, and I'm still here now … an old maid," she added, with a tinge of regret. A brief smile.

"I'm sorry to hear that, Melissa. That's tragic."

"My sister, meanwhile, had grown into a bit of a wild child. I expect you've seen photos of her?" Sharpe nodded. "She had the looks, and was a feisty madam … a real livewire. She had no intention of staying in Barnsley. When she was about eighteen, she posed for some glamour photos, and the next thing we knew was that she was in that *Penthouse magazine* and had moved to London. She lived there for nine or ten years. God knows what she got up to then. I only saw her at Christmas or at the occasional family wedding or funeral." She paused. "Then, one Christmas, she went to a party in a posh house in Leeds, I think, and that's where she met Arthur. He was completely bowled over, of course, and once she found out that he was stinking rich, she wrapped him around her little finger. She moved back to Yorkshire and they were married in no time.

I tried to tell her that she would have to change her lifestyle and settle down, but she just ignored me. It wasn't too long before she got bored with him, then she started going out on her own, meeting friends, and disappearing for weekends at first, then a week or two at a time. We tried to tell Arthur to leave her, to get divorced, but he ignored our advice and forgave her every time she came back." She paused. "He's been an old fool, Tim."

"When you say *We*, who do …?"

"Arthur's sister, his friends, you know."

"Hmm," Sharpe looked thoughtful. "When did you last see your sister, Melissa?"

"It would have been at New Year. Arthur and Phoebe always had a New Year's Eve party at their house … a few friends and family, one or two neighbours as well. It wasn't a rowdy affair," she added, grinning, "a meal, a few drinks, and fireworks after midnight. It was a bit of a Bartlett family tradition. I always stayed at their house … too far to drive back here, you know, and I left the following morning. Phoebe was still in bed."

"Have you heard from her since?" Melissa shook her head. "Have you any idea where she might be?"

"No idea, sorry. Have you checked out the friend who reported her missing?"

"Someone else from the team is dealing with that. Have you no idea where she may have gone?"

"I wish I could help, but as I told you earlier, we're not close. Phoebe doesn't confide in me." Sharpe drained his cup.

"OK, Melissa, I think that's all for now, but we may have to speak to you again." He stood up, and pointed down at the table. "Thanks for the tea and gingerbread. Very nice," he smiled. Melissa stood up quickly, and brushed past him to go into the kitchen.

"Here," she said, handing him a paper bag, "there's some more in there. You policemen are far too skinny," she added, smiling, as she moved towards the front door.

CHAPTER NINE

Ryan glanced at his watch. Nearly 8.30am. No sign of Bentley, nor of Sharpe. The door to the Incident Room opened, and Debbie Chapman backed her way in, carrying a tray of coffees. She was just about to allow the door to close as Bentley appeared, studying a notepad. Debbie handed out mugs to Ryan and Slater, and popped one on Bentley's desk as he opened the morning briefing.

"Apologies for the delay, folks, but Tim's wife has gone into labour and he's at the hospital. He's just phoned to tell me about his interview with Melissa Jordan, so I'll begin with that, while it's still fresh in my head. She's about ten years older than Phoebe Bartlett, is unmarried, and, according to Tim, is a bit of an old maid … a Plain Jane."

"I already knew that, Sir," Slater remarked, a slight smile on his face, "but I didn't want to spoil the surprise for Sharpie." Debbie Chapman grinned.

"Anyway, it sounds like there's no love lost between the sisters, and Melissa's long been disgusted by Phoebe's behaviour and wild lifestyle. She told

Arthur Bartlett to rein her in, or to divorce her, but he wouldn't listen. He just forgives his wife every time." He glanced down at his notes. "Melissa last saw Phoebe at the Bartletts' New Year party. A few close friends were there, together with some neighbours, and Melissa stayed over … too far to drive home at that late hour. She left in the morning without seeing her sister, who was still asleep, or hung over." He glanced down again. "I think that covers the main points, except that, according to Sharpe, she makes great gingerbread." A few smiles. "Any questions?"

"Did anything unusual happen at the party?" Ryan asked.

"Sharpe didn't mention anything, George, and neither did Barbara and Tom Galbraith, whom I interviewed yesterday. She's Arthur Bartlett's sister, and they live in a biggish house at Sleights, near Whitby. Tom Galbraith is a skipper on one of the local fishing trawlers, and he's at sea at the moment." Bentley paused, and flicked through his notepad. "Barbara Galbraith didn't have a lot to say, but I thought she seemed edgy … I think she would have preferred her husband to be there. She seemed anxious to get rid of me as quickly as possible, but from the little information she gave me, it was obvious that she doesn't like Phoebe and that she and her husband have little to do with the Bartletts. They did attend the party at Filey, but she reckoned that they left soon after midnight. She doesn't drink much, so she drove back to Whitby. I'll have interview her husband next week, but that's about all she had to tell us." He glanced at the others, then nodded to Debbie Chapman. "What did you find out, Debbie?"

"Harold Hardy, fifty-odd, a posh golfing mate of Bartlett, and another successful businessman. He's into men's fashion, and has shops in Scarborough, York and Leeds. He didn't beat about the bush, and told me that he's always thought that Phoebe is a gold-digging slapper and little more than a jumped-up whore."

"Typical Yorkshireman," Bentley muttered, "blunt, and straight to the point."

"Yeah," Chapman continued, "he reckoned that he warned Bartlett not to get too involved, and added that many of Bartlett's old friends steer well clear of him these days. Most of the wives are worried that Phoebe might try to get her claws into their husbands." Ryan and Slater laughed softly.

"She has got that sort of reputation in the family," Slater glanced at the others, "and that's why the Bartletts aren't invited to many of the family dos. I'm surprised that Mr Bartlett has put up with it for so long."

"Love's often blind," Chapman stated stoically.

"Hmm," Bentley mused, "did Hardy stay over at the house, Debbie?"

"No, Sir, he told me that he was pretty drunk, but was able to walk home. He lives in Filey, not too far away."

"OK, well I think we've all got the picture," Bentley said in summary. "The family don't like her, and aren't going to tell us much more. We need to interview the Bartletts' neighbours, and to see if they can add any more detail to what happened at that New Year party. George, Debbie, pop back to that estate after tea and find out which of the neighbours were at the party. Let's see what they have to say about the Bartletts' friends and family."

"What about Bartlett's security camera tapes, Sir?" Ryan asked. "Shall we pick them up so that they can be checked?"

"Good idea, son. All of the visitors should be on the most recent tape." He turned to Slater. "Dennis, will you do some background checks on the family members? Find out if any of them has any form, particularly in connection with Phoebe Bartlett." Slater nodded. "In the meantime, I'll nip down to the hospital and see if Sharpie's become a Daddy yet. We're chasing too many bloody shadows at the moment," he added gruffly. "I'll decide after tomorrow's briefing whether they're still worth pursuing." He headed for his office, followed by Chapman and Ryan.

"Sir," Chapman asked, "can we just have a quick word before you go to the hospital?"

"Sure, what is it?"

"It's about Fiona Charlton, Sir," Chapman continued, as she and Ryan pulled up a chair each and sat down. "George can tell you the story."

Bentley looked puzzled, and waited for Ryan to begin.

"I'll just give you a brief outline, Sir, then perhaps you can give us some advice. I think you know that Fiona and I saw each other during the summer?" Bentley nodded. "She's been staying at Debbie's for a while, but I have been seeing Fiona again since your party. She told me that she had a boyfriend called Gary Henderson in Liverpool some years ago … she was very keen on him, but then he was busted for drug-dealing in a big way, and has been in Strangeways ever since. He has a parole hearing this week."

"OK, George, so what's the problem? She went out with him years ago, so he's history."

"That's right, Sir, but the problem is that she betrayed him to the police, and was the main prosecution witness at his trial. A close friend of hers died after obtaining drugs from one of his contacts, so, even though she was in love with him, Fiona felt that she had to tell the police." Ryan glanced at Chapman.

"Fiona's really worried about what Henderson might do if he's released on parole, Sir," Chapman continued. "She's really happy here, but she's terrified that he might try to wreak some kind of revenge on her. What do you think, Sir? Can you find out any information from the authorities at Strangeways?" Bentley glanced at the photo on his desk, and scratched at the loose flesh on his neck.

"I can see why you are both concerned," he answered slowly, looking at each of them, "but I can't see Henderson trying to harm Fiona over here … or anywhere else, if it comes to that. There will be strict conditions on his movements if he is granted parole, you know. How long has he been in Strangeways?"

"About five years, Sir" Ryan replied.

"I can't see anyone in his right mind wanting to risk getting banged up for life after spending five years in there." Ryan still looked anxious. "OK, George, I've got to get to the hospital to see Tim, but I'll make some calls after that and let you know in the morning. OK?" he asked, standing up and reaching for his coat.

"Thanks, Sir," Chapman muttered, as she and Ryan stood up and Bentley hurried past them.

***

"Good evening, Mr Bartlett," Chapman spoke into the intercom, "it's DS Chapman and DC Ryan from Scarborough Police. May we speak with you again?" The door buzzed and opened slightly. They walked along the gravelled driveway to the front entrance where a grim-faced Arthur Bartlett was waiting for them.

"I thought I made myself clear when we spoke before," he said gruffly.

"We just have one or two more questions, Mr Bartlett," Chapman replied sharply. "May we come in?" Bartlett stood aside and ushered them in to the lounge. Ryan remained standing as Chapman eased herself into one of the comfortable armchairs.

"Have you heard from your wife since our last visit, Mr Bartlett?"

"No, as I told you, she could be away for some time, particularly if she has gone searching for some winter sunshine." A thin smile.

"You told us that some of your neighbours attended your New Year party, Mr Bartlett. Would you give us their names and addresses, please?" Ryan opened his notepad.

"I fail to see why you need to involve them, DS Chapman. As I have already made clear, my wife often goes away without telling me where she is going. I have not reported her as being missing, so is this an official investigation?"

"Not as yet, Mr Bartlett, but your wife was last seen on the third of January. It is now the seventeenth. Surely you must be a little worried by now? We are certainly concerned, Mr Bartlett, concerned enough to extend our enquiries, so please, may I have the details I requested?" Bartlett looked furious as he grabbed Ryan's notepad and scribbled some names and addresses. He thrust the pad back into Ryan's hand.

"This is a total waste of time, officer. I can't see how these people can help you. I don't like my neighbours being dragged into my personal affairs."

"If that's the case, Mr Bartlett," Chapman answered shrilly, standing up and glaring at him, "you should keep a tighter rein on your wife's movements, then we wouldn't have to waste a lot of valuable time chasing around and trying to find out where she is. It's our duty to show concern if somebody appears to be missing, even if you don't seem to be bothered." She made to leave, but paused as Ryan spoke.

"Your security tape, Mr Bartlett," he asked, "may we borrow it?"

"Of course, but after your last visit I re-wound it slightly before starting the tape running again. The footage you saw has been erased, I'm afraid." Ryan turned to look at Chapman.

"We'd still like to take the tape for examination, Mr Bartlett," she said. Ryan waited for Bartlett to return, pushed the tape into his pocket and followed Chapman to the front door.

"Thank you for your time, Mr Bartlett," she said. "We'll be in touch again … soon." She and Ryan crunched across the driveway, opened the gate and walked to their car. Bartlett stood on the gravel outside the porch until the outer gate was closed, then he locked the front door, returned to the lounge, and reached for the phone.

***

Chapman and Ryan sat in the car, studying Ryan's notepad by torchlight. "It's too cold to be hanging around, George, so let's see where these people live."

"Mostly on this estate, Debbie, by the look of it. There's only a handful of houses here, so the Bartletts probably invite all of their neighbours. We may as well knock on every door. Let's start across there," he pointed.

***

"Two down, two to go," Chapman muttered, rubbing her hands together to get them warm. "Nobody at home in the first house, then the old couple at the end house didn't have much to tell us, eh George?"

"No, I got the impression that they don't do a lot of socialising, Debbie. They only stayed at the party for an hour … less even. They hardly knew the Bartletts. Let's hope that we have more joy at that house on the other side of *Mandalay*. When we were here the other day, I saw a woman with a young girl." They crossed the roadway to another ornate metal gateway, opened it and headed for a brightly-lit porch. Ryan glanced at his frosty breath as Chapman rang the bell. The door was opened by a tall man, fortyish, with thinning dark hair.

"Good evening, Sir," Chapman held out her warrant card, "I'm DS Chapman and this is DC Ryan. We're from North Yorkshire Police. I'm sorry to interrupt your evening, but may we come in and have a few words with you and your wife?"

"Of course," he stood aside, then closed the door. "Please, we're through there." They walked into a large, modern lounge, where his wife moved to greet them. "Helen, it's the police." She looked puzzled, then ushered them into the room.

"Please, find a seat," she smiled, pointing to a large settee, on the opposite side of the room to the TV, where a young boy and girl were watching a Disney cartoon. "Robin," she called to the boy, "the

TV's too loud. Turn it down." She turned back to Chapman and Ryan. "Tea or coffee?"

"One of each, please," Chapman replied, watching as she headed for the kitchen. "We'll wait until your wife returns. Is it Mr Archer?"

"Yes, I'm Stuart, then there's my wife Helen, son Robin, and daughter Amelia." He smiled. "Let's go into the kitchen, away from the children." He led the way to a large pine table, and they sat down as Mrs Archer placed a tray on the table.

"Please help yourself," she spoke quickly, smiling. "What's all this about?" she asked, glancing anxiously at her husband.

"Nothing to get worried about, Mrs Archer," Chapman smiled, "we've called here to ask you a few questions about your neighbours, the Bartletts."

"Arthur and Phoebe, they're nice … we get on well with them, don't we, Stuart? Is there something wrong?"

"We're not sure," Chapman replied, sipping her coffee. "This is confidential, you understand?" Mrs Archer nodded. "We received a report from one of Mrs Bartlett's friends that she hasn't been seen for some time, and we are concerned that she might be missing."

"Phoebe missing, surely that can't be?" Mrs Archer muttered. "It's not that long since we last saw her." She glanced at her husband. "We were at a party at their house on New Year's Eve, weren't we, Stuart?"

"Yes, that's right," he continued. "The Bartletts

always throw a party for family and friends on New Year's Eve, and they have fireworks. The kids love it," he added, grinning.

"We haven't seen her since then," Mrs Archer took up the story, "but I seem to remember Arthur saying something about a holiday. Phoebe often goes away for a weekend break, or longer. She doesn't work, and Arthur doesn't travel well these days, so it's not unusual for her to go off on her own, is it, Stuart?"

"Yes, she seems to be a bit of a free spirit."

"The other thing is … well, I don't want to appear to be a gossip, DS Chapman, but Phoebe is quite a bit younger than Arthur, and I think she has her own circle of friends." Stuart Archer gave his wife a disapproving look.

"Perhaps, Helen, but they always seem to get on well, don't they?"

"Oh yes, and Phoebe absolutely adores Amelia, our daughter, and is always making a fuss of her. She hasn't any children of her own, you see."

"Right," Debbie Chapman took advantage of a pause in the conversation, "I think we get the picture. Can you tell us who was at the Bartletts' party?" Ryan prepared to take notes.

"We didn't really speak much to their family and friends," Helen Archer answered, "except Melissa, Phoebe's sister. I had a chat with her, but I couldn't tell you who the others were. They kept to themselves. As for the neighbours, Mr and Mrs Bond from the end house were there, but they didn't stay long. The

Grants were there, and the Irvines," she paused to think for a few seconds, "oh, and Frank Parkinson from the farm up the road."

"Mr Bartlett didn't mention him," Ryan muttered, studying his notepad.

"Well, he was definitely there, and so were Robin and Amelia. It was a bit late for them, but they were on holiday and Phoebe let them play games all evening, then we left after the fireworks. Most of the others were still there when we left, I think."

"Yes, that's true," added her husband. "The fireworks were great this year. Amelia made some superb sketches the day after."

"How would you describe the atmosphere?" Chapman asked.

"A little formal," Mr Archer replied, "but it was pleasant, no drunken arguments." They laughed.

"What about Phoebe … did she seem to be enjoying herself?"

"She seemed alright," Helen Archer answered thoughtfully, "though to be honest, I don't think there's a lot of love lost between her and some of the family."

"You're gossiping again, love." She smirked.

"Would you mind if we have a quick word with the children?" Chapman asked.

"If you like," Helen replied, "but Robin won't be able to tell you much, apart from how good the fireworks were, and I'm afraid Amelia won't be able to tell you anything."

"Oh, why's that?"

"She's a deaf mute, DS Chapman," she replied, glancing at the children in the lounge then turning back to the policewoman. "She can't speak at all."

CHAPTER TEN

Bentley drained his mug of coffee, placed it noisily on his desk, sat down then looked at Chapman, Slater and Ryan in turn. "Tim's the proud father of a little girl," he smiled widely, "and we're all invited to the Turk's Head pub on Saturday night to wet the baby's head!" Grins all around.

"That's great news, Sir," Chapman remarked, "let's hope that Sharpie settles down now and shows a bit more maturity, you know, a bit more consideration for others."

"Bloody Hell, Debbie," Bentley laughed, "he's got a baby girl, not a personality transplant! He's not going to grow a halo anytime soon, you can bet on that."

"Give him a chance, Sir, let's wait and see," muttered the quiet Slater. "His life is bound to change, so let's hope it's for the better."

"I'm with the DI on this one," Ryan said, "a leopard doesn't change its spots, but I have to say that it would be nice if he would get off my back in the future."

"He's only jealous of you, George," Debbie Chapman touched his arm gently, "because you're bright and you'll go far in this job, but Tim's a decent copper and perhaps having a daughter will make him realise that there are things in life far more important than promotions or chasing women."

"Maybe," Bentley nodded thoughtfully, "and we can enjoy a good night out on Saturday, but in the meantime we need to locate Phoebe Bartlett. Any joy with the neighbours, Debbie?"

"Not a great deal, Sir. Most of them were at the party on New Year's Eve, but they didn't stay until the end and couldn't tell us much about Phoebe's family. The Archers who live next door to the Bartletts were the most helpful, and they confirmed that Phoebe often goes off on her own. They told us that she really dotes on their daughter Amelia, who is deaf and dumb, and they spend a lot of time together. The little girl is a fantastic artist though, isn't she, George?"

"Yes, I had a look through her latest sketch-book, and she's drawn two or three impressive portraits of Phoebe Bartlett, plus lots of animal sketches, drawings of nearby buildings, and so on. She's a sweet little girl, really friendly, despite her handicap." He glanced at the others. "She communicates by sign language." The DI raised his eyebrows.

"Very nice," Bentley nodded, "but did you find any new information, Debbie?"

"Just one thing, Sir, that Frank Parkinson, who lives in the farm nearby, was also at the party. Bartlett never mentioned him when we asked for names of the neighbours who attended the party."

"There's something else, Sir," Ryan continued, "Bartlett's wiped some of the security tape, so we've lost the footage of Phoebe Bartlett loading her car and leaving the house on the third of January."

"That's a pain," Bentley grunted, searching for a jelly-baby in his pocket.

"I've brought the tape," Ryan got up and placed it on the DI's desk, "so there might still be something useful on it." Bentley picked it up, then turned to Slater.

"Get this checked out, Dennis, will you, and see if we've got anything on that farmer … Parkinson, isn't it?"

"Frank Parkinson," Chapman muttered. "He lives at Lamb Rigg Farm, Dennis."

"Cheers."

"Right, that's all for now. Debbie, George, go and have a word with that farmer, OK? One last thing, Tim will be back in tomorrow." Bentley eased himself up from his chair and headed for his office. He stopped and gestured towards Chapman and Ryan. They followed him into his office. "Before you go, I phoned through to Strangeways and spoke to the Governor. He told me that the hearing is next Tuesday, and that he expects Henderson to be freed on the following Friday. There's nothing to prevent it, apparently. Henderson has been a model prisoner, and he's shown remorse for the crimes he committed, and blames himself for turning Fiona against him. He reckons that she was the love of his life, but has accepted that she's moved on and wishes her well. He's convinced the authorities that he's a changed man, and they don't regard him as a threat. I think that's all, George."

"Thanks for that, Sir," Ryan smiled briefly.

"Let's hope they're right, George," Chapman muttered, "and that he's trying to be a good man, and not a good actor."

***

"I think that's everything that Bentley told us, Fiona," Ryan spoke softly on the phone. "The parole hearing is on Tuesday, and it's pretty certain that Henderson will be a free man next Friday." Silence. "Are you OK?"

"Yes, I'm alright, George. I guess I've been dreading to hear this news, but it had to happen sometime. They can't keep Gary locked up for ever."

"The most important thing is to get on with our lives, Fi. If the release is confirmed on Tuesday, I can then find out the conditions attached to it, but we have to move on. You can't allow Henderson to dictate the rest of your life."

"I understand what you are saying, George, but right now it's difficult for me to see beyond Tuesday."

"Everything will be fine, believe me. You have so much support here, from people who love you, so you have nothing to worry about." Another silence. "Anyway, listen … I have a surprise for you, Fiona. A few of the lads are meeting Tim Sharpe in town on Saturday night to celebrate the birth of his daughter, and I'm going to go along just to show my face, but later I'm going to pick you up and take you for a luxury overnight stay."

"That's great, George, something to cheer me up, thanks. Where are we going?"

"You'll have to wait and see, love … it's a surprise, but you will enjoy it and we'll be able to have some "us" time together, OK?"

"Thanks, George," she replied, sounding more

relaxed, "something nice to look forward to."

"I'll pick you up just before eight, so pack your toothbrush and be ready for a good time!" She laughed. "In the meantime, we're still looking for Phoebe Bartlett. Debbie and I have to interview a farmer tomorrow, but I have a feeling that we've got more than a Missing Person on our hands."

"Yes, Debbie told me that it's not looking good … that it's been too long with no clues about her whereabouts." She paused. "At least you have an interesting case to occupy your time. I've probably got a routine, boring day at Whitby tomorrow, and the same again on Saturday, with too much time to think."

"Come on, Fi, we've been through that. Think about our weekend together. I'll give you a clue … Eboracum."

"Eboracum, where the hell's that?"

"You've got a day or so to find out, love," he laughed. "See you on Saturday around eight."

CHAPTER ELEVEN

Debbie Chapman slowed down as she approached the small estate of luxury homes where the Bartletts lived, and Ryan glanced down to his left at a rough hand-painted wooden sign resting against a large stone on the roadside:

The road narrowed as it passed the ornate gateways and manicured lawns of the houses, and quickly became a lane, then little more than a rough trackway, potholed and scarred by the movement of the farm tractor. Chapman swerved suddenly to avoid a shallow dip near a gateway to a field, where numerous cowpats were spread across the lane. "You can wash the car when we get back," she grinned at Ryan, as she swung the car again to miss another large patch.

"Cheers, Debbie," Ryan muttered, "I once worked on a farm during the summer holidays when I was at university. It took me ages to get rid of the stink!" Chapman eased the car round a sharp bend, and Ryan sat up and peered at a cluster of buildings a hundred yards or so ahead of them. "Welcome to Lamb Rigg Farm," he glanced at Chapman, then was jostled in his seat as she tried to avoid another pothole.

"If I hit one of these bloody holes," she barked, "the car won't make it back to the station." She slowed down and headed for the building which she thought might be the farmhouse. "What a dump! I don't think we'll be treated to a farmhouse tea with jam and scones here, George!" She pulled the car into a small yard, where an ageing Land Rover was parked outside a sturdy-looking wooden door. Chapman parked the car nearby, and as Ryan exited on the other side, a collie appeared. It was tethered to a long rope, and barked fiercely as they approached the doorway.

"I like dogs," Ryan remarked, "but I'm not going near this one."

"Very wise," Chapman muttered, wrapping her chewing-gum in a small piece of paper, then keeping her eye on the dog as she hammered on the wooden door. A couple of minutes passed before the door was opened by a tall, well-built man with dark unkempt hair.

"Give over, Tess," he shouted at the dog, "get back in your kennel." He watched as the dog calmed down, then he turned to Chapman and Ryan.

"What do you want?" he asked bluntly.

"We're from North Yorkshire Police, Mr Parkinson," Chapman spoke sternly, "and we'd like to have a word with you."

"A word about what?" Parkinson asked, glancing at their warrant cards.

"About whom, Mr Parkinson. We need to have a chat with you about Phoebe Bartlett." He peered around the farmyard. "May we…?" she gestured towards the door. Parkinson turned and pushed the door open, as Chapman and Ryan looked at each other then followed him into the dark house. They passed along a narrow hallway before entering a large, dimly-lit lounge, where an elderly lady was slouched in an armchair, partly buried by a couple of cats.

"Who are these people?" she asked meekly.

"We're from …" Chapman began.

"No-one that you need to be bothered about, Mother," Parkinson interrupted sharply, "we'll be in the kitchen."

"Shall I make …?"

"No need, Mother, they won't be staying." He gestured for Chapman and Ryan to follow him, and pointed at two chairs under a rough farmhouse table, which was cluttered with papers and dirty pots. He gathered the pots and placed them in the sink, pushed the papers to one end of the table, then sat down opposite the two police officers. "Phoebe Bartlett," he said gruffly, looking at each officer in turn, "what about her?"

"She's been reported as being missing, Mr Parkinson," Chapman replied, "and we'd like to know when you last saw her." Parkinson thought for a moment.

"New Year's Eve, at her house," he answered slowly. "The Bartletts always have a party at their house on New Year's Eve, and they usually invite a few neighbours and some of their relatives."

"Can you tell me which neighbours, which relatives, Mr Parkinson?"

"I don't rightly know, Miss …"

"DS Chapman, and this is DC Ryan."

"OK, as I was saying, I didn't take much notice of who was there. I didn't stay that long." He paused for a moment. "Phoebe's sister was there, and some of Mr Bartlett's friends, I think, then there were a few neighbours. I don't really know them. That couple with the deaf and dumb girl were there … you probably know them, the girl's always drawing things. I think they live next door to the Bartletts." Ryan nodded.

"Were there any arguments?" he asked.

"Not that I saw," Parkinson replied. "It was all very polite. It always is, pretty boring if you ask me. Most people left after the fireworks."

"Do you know the Bartletts well, Mr Parkinson?" Chapman asked. "If you don't mind my saying, you don't really look their type."

"Not posh enough?" he laughed. Ryan smiled. "Well, you can't always judge a book by its cover, lass. I've probably got more money that the lot of them put together. Just because I look like one of them Dingles off that Emmerdale programme doesn't mean that I'm poor."

"How long have you known the Bartletts?"

"Eight or ten years, perhaps. When my father passed away, I decided to give up running the farm. I was never really interested," he added, looking at Ryan, "and Mother was becoming frail, so I sold off a lot of our land to property developers, you see. I used to own the land where the Bartletts and the others live, those big houses down the lane, and as for the rest of the farmland, well I've rented it off to the Jacksons, who run Park Farm, a mile or two away."

"How do you spend your time now, Mr Parkinson, as you're still relatively young?" Chapman asked.

"I look after Mother of course, and in the summer months I do a bit of gardening, some building, you know, an odd job here and there. As I told you before, I don't need the money. It's just something to pass the time."

"OK, thank you, and you're certain that you haven't seen Phoebe Bartlett since New Year?"

"No, I last saw her at the party."

"How do you get on with her?" Ryan asked quietly.

"Well enough, I suppose. She was friendly with most people, you know," he paused in thought, then he laughed and added, "aye, she's a friendly person … very lively, some say. Mr Bartlett is far too quiet for her, I think." He thought again for a moment, then looked up. "Now, is that it? Have you got all of the information that you want, because I'll need to see to Mother?" He stood up.

"I think that's all for now, Mr Parkinson,"
Chapman replied, "you've been very helpful … thanks for your time." She and Ryan stood up and made ready to go, then Ryan turned to ask a final question.

"Oh, one last thing, have you seen her car recently, Mr Parkinson?"

"No, can't say that I have. She was always here and there in that car, sometimes for days. She's probably somewhere in it now." He headed back into the lounge, leaving the two officers to find their own way out. Ryan followed Chapman to the car, glancing around at the other buildings around the yard, then he opened the passenger door and got in.

"Well, what do you reckon, George?"

"A bit of a mystery man, Debbie, a rough diamond, and I think there's quite a lot that he hasn't told us."

"What do you mean?"

"Well, for example, why would Arthur Bartlett and his posh friends want to have such a rough character at the party?"

"Probably because he looked after their gardens, and after all, he is a neighbour."

"Maybe, but would you invite your dustbinman to your Christmas do?" They both laughed, then Chapman started the engine and edged the car slowly out of the farmyard.

CHAPTER TWELVE

George Ryan found a parking space close to Eastborough, locked his car and hurried down the sloping hill towards the Old Town. It was drizzling lightly, and he shrugged his jacket over his head to keep dry. He could see the lights of the Turk's Head in the distance, and as he neared the pub the noise grew stronger. Ryan stepped into the porch, pulled down his jacket and straightened his hair, then opened the door just as a young couple lurched into him, then staggered outside, laughing. Ryan glanced at his watch. Drunk before 7.30pm! He grinned briefly as he watched them swaying up the hill, then he headed towards the long bar, searching for Sharpe's party crowd. He spotted Debbie Chapman and Don Bentley at the end of the bar, eased past some other drinkers, and stood quietly behind Bentley, who was passing a tenner to the barman. "Just in time," he shouted in Bentley's ear, "mine's a pint, Sir."

"Good timing as usual, George," Bentley grunted, as he turned back to the barman. "Take another out of that, please."

"You're late," Chapman scolded, "everyone's been here since seven."

"Sorry, Debbie, I was just getting a few last-minute things together. How's Fiona?"

"Good … looking forward to your surprise. I hope she's not disappointed, George."

"She won't be," he grinned. "Oh, cheers, Sir," as Bentley shoved a pint in his direction. "Where's Sharpie?" he muttered, taking a drink.

"We're over in that far corner, George. Just head for the noise." Bentley led the way, and Ryan could see Tim Sharpe clinging onto one of his friends, laughing loudly. He broke away as Ryan approached.

"I'm going for a piss," he announced loudly, then paused as he saw Ryan with the others. "Bloody Hell," he spluttered, "if it isn't young George coming out to play with the big boys and girls!" Laughter.

"Congratulations, Tim," Ryan held out his hand, "I'm glad that everything went fine for you and Laura." Sharpe paused.

"Cheers, George," he shook Ryan's hand, then hugged him enthusiastically. "I appreciate that. We've got a beautiful little daughter," he added, releasing Ryan from his grip. "I feel great … really proud. Someday you'll know what I mean," then he smiled and whispered in Ryan's ear, "someday soon, perhaps, if those dicky birds' tales about you and the delicious Fiona are true." He laughed loudly, then clutched his groin. "Shit … gotta go," he muttered as he scurried towards the toilets. Ryan looked at Chapman and Bentley and smiled briefly, taking another gulp of his beer. He turned to chat to two of the local PCs.

"How is Fiona, Debbie?" Bentley asked.

"Putting on a brave face, Sir. She's still edgy about Henderson's release, but she seems more determined now to get on with her life." She looked across where Ryan was still deep in conversation. "She's pretty keen on our George, you know."

"Is that right, Debbie?" He paused. "By the way, there's something I didn't tell you after I had that chat with the Governor at Strangeways."

"What's that, Sir?"

"Fiona Charlton visited Henderson in Strangeways every week for the first two years after he was banged up."

***

George Ryan checked the traffic to his right, then eased his car off the A64, heading for the centre of Scarborough. "So," he muttered, smiling, "have you enjoyed our little escape to York, Fiona?"

"Last night was lovely, George … and this morning. It was a real treat," she beamed, touching his arm gently. "You're getting better," she added, and they both laughed. "No, seriously, it's been a nice break, George – good food, a little together time, and I even enjoyed the cultural bits. I'm not a history buff like you, but the Castle Museum was great."

"Yeah, I enjoyed it too. It's a while since I was there." He slowed as the traffic built up in the outskirts of the town. "I've a feeling that the DI will have a busy day planned for us tomorrow, so I'll just drop you at the door and catch up tomorrow night. Is that OK?"

"Fine, George. There's that film I want to see … Titanic. It's on at the Hollywood Plaza, and Monday evening should be quiet. Do you fancy it?"

"No problem, Fi. I'll check out the starting times, and give you a ring around teatime." He wound the window down and watched as she headed into the house. "Sleep tight," he called and waved, before driving off into the night.

CHAPTER THIRTEEN

Tuesday afternoon. The search for Phoebe Bartlett had been put on the back burner, as there had been an attempted armed break-in at a house in Weaponness, on the outskirts of Scarborough. Two thieves had managed to enter the house and had gathered some valuables, before being disturbed by the elderly occupant, a lady in her seventies. She had been woken by noises from downstairs and had phoned the police, before going downstairs to investigate. In the melee which followed, she had been wounded by one of the robbers, a teenager who was well-known to Bentley and his team, and, recovering in hospital, she was able to identify him when Chapman and Bentley showed her some photos on Tuesday morning. The team were able to make two quick arrests by lunchtime, and had spent the rest of the afternoon taking witness statements. Bentley gathered the team together for a short briefing before they headed home.

"Well, for once, that was an easy operation," he

muttered philosophically. “I wish every victim was as tough as old Mrs Thompson. We could do with a few recruits like her,” he added, smiling. “Debbie and I will interview the two young lads in the morning, then we'll pay a visit to Arthur Bartlett at one of his shops in the afternoon. I want the rest of you to concentrate on our search for Phoebe Bartlett. We need to double-check the information given by those relatives who were at the party, and to see if any of them has heard from Phoebe. I need to know when that trawler skipper … Galbraith isn't it? … is back on shore, so that we can interview him more thoroughly too. Tim … get in touch with Leeds CID and ask them to call at that footballer's house. We need to find out if he has any more information for us, but I also want to make sure that Phoebe isn't hiding at his place and giving us the runaround. When you've done that, I want you and Dennis to catch up with that mate of Bartlett's … Hardy, isn't it? Put some pressure on him, and see what reaction you get. Find out how much time he and Bartlett spend with each other, OK?” Dennis Slater nodded and glanced at Sharpe, as Bentley continued. “George, you can have another word with the Archer family. They seemed to know more about the goings-on around the Bartlett's house. The other neighbours are too senile.” One or two sniggers. “When you've done that, drive out to Osmotherley and have a word with some of Melissa Jordan's neighbours. Find out if she's had any new visitors recently, OK? Don't bother questioning her again,

George … we can bring her in if necessary when we've assessed the information from the others." He glanced around the room. "We've spent enough time pussyfooting around this case, so tomorrow I want to put more pressure on Arthur Bartlett and the others and see what happens. He hasn't even bothered to contact us to see if we've turned up any clues about his wife's disappearance. I don't like it. Even if his wife was a fire-breathing dragon, most husbands would have shown some interest." He dug into his pocket for a jelly-baby. "OK, that's enough for today. Get yourselves home, but I'm warning you … tomorrow's going to be a busy day!" There was a flurry of coats and *Goodbyes*. "Oh, George," Bentley called across the room, "just a quick word before you go." Ryan walked over to the DI's desk. "I had a call from Manchester, George. Gary Henderson is going to be released on parole on Friday." Ryan smiled briefly and nodded. "Thought you'd want to know." Ryan nodded again, grabbed his jacket and headed for the door.

***

"Hi Fiona, how's things?" George asked.

"Fine, George, I'm just relaxing after my tea. We've had a busy day at Whitby. A couple who were caught shoplifting in an antiques centre, then a young lad was bitten by a dog, and to cap it all an elderly chap lost his footing near the harbour wall and fell in."

"Christ, poor devil, it must have been freezing."

"Yeah, we couldn't save him. By the time we managed to fish him out, he'd gone." She paused. "Not a nice way to go," she added.

"No, horrible. Are you OK?"

"Fine, George, just a bit tired."

"Get your feet up and watch a bit of telly," he said, laughing softly. "*Titanic* was great last night."

"Don't beat about the bush, George. Tell me why you are calling."

"Gary Henderson is going to be released on Friday morning." Silence. "The Boss told me earlier, and said that you haven't got to worry." Silence. "Fiona?"

"Don't worry, I'm still here, and so is Debbie." She paused. "We both knew it was going to happen, George, so there's little point in getting worked up about it. I've just got to get on with my life."

"Exactly, and don't forget … you've got friends who will support you, so if there's anything at all that's bugging you, just speak out. I'll always be here, Fi, so don't forget … I love you. We've got to look to the future, not the past."

"You're right, George, and I'll probably feel better soon, now that I know what's going to happen. I'll be fine … we'll be fine, OK?"

"Too true. Anyway, we'll catch up and have a drink tomorrow. I'll call for you about eight."

"That's good, George. I'll look forward to it. Love you too," she added, as she put the phone down.

CHAPTER FOURTEEN

Ryan drained his coffee, dipped a slice of bread in his egg and ate a few more chips. He glanced out of the window, saw that it had stopped raining, and quickly finished his meal. He gestured to the waitress, who shuffled across to his table.

"Would you like a pudding?"

"No, thank you, I'm full," Ryan smiled, patting his tummy. "That was lovely, thanks. Have you the bill, please?" He followed her to the counter and gave her a £5 note. "Keep the change, love." He grabbed his coat, and headed outside, zipping his coat tight as the chilly breeze hit him. Ryan walked slowly along the Crescent, gazing over the rough sea to Filey Brigg, and thinking back to his conversation with Mrs Archer earlier that morning. She had chatted more freely now that her husband was at work, and her children at school.

"Amelia attends a school near York which specialises in teaching deaf mutes," she had explained.

"I stayed in York with a friend a few days ago," Ryan added. "Fiona hadn't been there before, but she really enjoyed our brief stay."

"Yes, there's so much to see."

"We're still looking for any clues which may help us locate Mrs Bartlett," Ryan continued, "and I've called here today to see if you had remembered anything else." She ushered him into the lounge, where he sank into one of the armchairs.

"I think I told you the names of all of the guests at the party."

"What about other times, Mrs Archer? Were the Bartletts good neighbours? Did they seem to get on well with each other?"

"Difficult to say, DC Ryan."

"Please call me George."

"OK, George, as I was saying, it's difficult to give you much information, as we didn't see the Bartletts together all that often. Arthur was busy with his shops, and he liked to play golf, so we didn't see much of him. As for Phoebe, well ... she didn't spend a lot of time in the house, you know, she was often away, sometimes for a few days at a time. I think they were civil with the other neighbours, but that was all. The only time they invited their neighbours into *Mandalay* was at New Year, but members of their family called occasionally, sometimes when Phoebe was away."

"Did they have any other regular callers?"

"Just the usual ... the postman, that kind of

thing." She paused, then smiled. "Mr Parkinson from the farm used to do some gardening for them, but that stopped a year or two ago."

"Why are you smiling?"

"Well, I did hear a whisper, you know, some tittle-tattle that he only worked at the house when Mr Bartlett was at work or playing golf." She laughed lightly. "It was probably just local gossip, you know … happens everywhere, but I do remember that someone once pinned a piece of cardboard over the sign for Lamb Rigg Farm."

"A piece of cardboard? That's a bit odd."

"Yes, but it had a new name, George … **LIMP PRICK FARM**," she giggled, placing her hand over her mouth. Ryan smiled. "It only lasted a day or two, before Parkinson must have removed it."

"Hmm … interesting … so who does the gardening now?"

"Phoebe does most of it. They had a lot of the lawns replaced with paving and decking, so there's not as much work to do now."

"Right, that's helpful, Mrs Archer." He paused. "When I called here with DS Chapman, Amelia showed me some of her sketches. Do you think I could borrow her book?"

"Of course, unless she's taken it to school. Just a minute." She disappeared upstairs, returning a couple of minutes later holding a sketchpad. "I think this is the one you need, George. I noticed a sketch of the fireworks display, and some nice portraits of

Phoebe." She showed him one of the portraits, and handed the book to Ryan.

"Thanks, I'll take good care of it."

"Don't worry, George," she muttered, grinning, "Amelia's already started another!" Ryan stood up.

"You've been very helpful, Mrs Archer. I hope we won't have to bother you again, but I will return Amelia's sketchbook as soon as I can."

"That's fine," she replied, guiding Ryan to the front door. "So you've still no firm news about Phoebe?" she asked, frowning.

"Not really, Mrs Archer, but I'm sure that we'll have some answers soon."

"I hope so, George. Amelia misses her terribly."

"Fingers crossed," Ryan muttered as he walked away.

***

Ryan parked near the market cross at Osmotherley, and walked the short distance to North End, where Melissa Jordan lived. The clouds hung low, and were dark and threatening towards the moors. He fastened his coat, took note of Melissa's house, then began knocking on some of the doors on the opposite side of the road. There was no reply at the first two houses, but the third door was opened by an elderly lady holding a large ginger cat.

"Can I help you, dear?"

"I'm sorry to bother you, madam," Ryan replied, showing her his warrant card. "I'm DC Ryan from

North Yorkshire Police, and I'd like to ask you a couple of questions."

"A policeman?" Ryan nodded. "Oh, please come in and find a seat." Another cat brushed against him as he moved into the small lounge. It jumped onto his knee as Ryan sat down. "Would you like a cup of tea?"

"I'm fine, Mrs …?"

"It's Miss Travers."

"OK Miss Travers, have you lived at Osmotherley for long?"

"All of my life, DC Ryan. This was my parents' house, and my family have lived in the village for generations. They used to be miners."

"That's interesting, Miss Travers." He paused. "I'd like to ask you a few confidential questions … "she looked puzzled "… so you haven't got to tell anyone. It's a secret between you and me. Is that OK, Miss Travers?"

"Oh yes, it's quite exciting, isn't it?" She relaxed back in her seat. "What kind of questions?"

"Do you know Melissa Jordan?"

"Of course, I know her well. She lives more or less directly across the road."

"What can you tell me about her?"

"She's not a local, but she has lived here for many years. She was courting, actually I think she was engaged to a local lad called Keith Danson, but he died tragically and soon afterwards she moved up here. I think she's from Sheffield, or somewhere near there."

"Barnsley."

"Yes, that's right, Barnsley. It's near Sheffield, isn't it?"

"Yes, not too far away. Well, Miss Travers, we are searching for a missing person … Melissa Jordan's sister."

"I've met her, DC Ryan, she's blonde … Phoebe?"

"Yes, that's right, well done. Have you seen her recently?"

"No, not for a long time. I don't think they got on well with each other. I've seen her car here occasionally, but not for a good year or so." She sipped her tea. "As I said before, I don't think they were close." She paused for another sip. "Are you sure you wouldn't like a cup of tea, or a coffee? It's such a cold day."

"OK, yes please, Miss Travers, you've persuaded me. May I have a coffee?"

"Of course, just give me a minute." The ginger cat joined the other one on Ryan's knee until Miss Travers returned a few minutes later.

"Shoo!" she exclaimed, chasing them off. "They always make a fuss of strangers." She headed back into the kitchen and returned with a tray. "Here's your coffee, and there's some biscuits and gingerbread. Please help yourself." Ryan laughed softly. "What's the matter?"

“Sorry, it’s just the gingerbread. Does everyone make it around here?”

“Oh, so you’ve already visited Melissa, have you? She always wins the annual competition at the village show.”

“A colleague of mine interviewed Melissa Jordan, and told us that her gingerbread was good,” Ryan replied, taking a bite at a generous chunk,” but yours is great too,” he added quickly. He sipped his coffee, then continued. “You mentioned Phoebe’s car, Miss Travers. Have you seen any other strange cars here, or anyone else who has visited Melissa occasionally?”

“You said that this conversation is just between you and me, didn’t you, DC Ryan?”

“Yes, of course, anything you tell me is totally confidential.”

“It’s just that I don’t want to let Melissa, or anyone else, think that I’ve been spying on her.” Ryan waited patiently. “Well, I did notice a gentleman visiting her a few times last year … probably more towards the end of the year. He always walks to her house and she leaves the door open for him, but one time I did see him parking a large posh car way up the street.” Ryan drained his coffee.

“How would you describe this gentleman, Miss Travers?”

“Tall, quite handsome I suppose … he was middle-aged I would say, perhaps mid-fifties or even sixty.”

“I see … and his car?”

“Oh, I haven’t a clue what kind. I don’t drive, you see. As I told you before, it was big and looked posh … expensive, you know.”

“Can you remember the colour?” She paused in thought.

“I only saw it the once, but I think it was green … yes green.

“That’s very helpful, Miss Travers. Have you noticed any other regular visitors who were not locals?”

“Not regular … I remember that a couple called, perhaps last November. I didn’t recognise them, and I don’t think I saw their car.”

“How would you describe them?”

“Oh, I can’t say. I only caught a glimpse. They weren’t young though.” Ryan waited while she continued to think.

“Is that everything, Miss Travers?” he smiled.

“I think so. I’m sorry, but my memory’s not what it used to be.”

“Don’t worry, Miss Travers, you’ve been very helpful, believe me. I might call again with some photos. Would that be OK?”

“Oh yes, anytime. I’ve enjoyed talking to you,” she grinned, “just like Inspector Morse, and I don’t often have handsome young men calling to see me.” Ryan smiled.

“Well, as I said before, I’ll probably call back with some photos … just to double-check, you understand?”

"Of course. I'll look forward to it, and don't worry … I won't tell Melissa Jordan that you've interviewed me." Ryan stood up and prepared to leave.

"Thank you again … and for the coffee and gingerbread … it was lovely. You ought to enter some in the annual competition and who knows, you might beat Melissa Jordan!"

"Fat chance," she scowled, "she always wins."

CHAPTER FIFTEEN

Light spots of rain dotted DCI Jefferson's jacket as he stood outside Jack Mason's detached house in Horsforth, Leeds. Jefferson took a brown envelope from his inside pocket and glanced at the other three police officers alongside him. It was seven-thirty in the morning. "Ready?" he muttered. The others nodded as he rang the bell. He waited a few minutes and rang it again. A light was switched on in the hall, then Jack Mason opened the door. He was wearing a blue dressing gown, but little else, and hadn't combed his hair. He blinked at the four police officers, then muttered gruffly:

"What do you want?"

"Jack Mason?" A grunt. "We have a warrant to search this house," Jefferson stated firmly, flicking the sheet of paper in front of Mason's eyes as he brushed past him, swiftly followed by the others.

"What the fuck!" Mason shouted angrily, turning to follow them. "You can't just …" The officers split up, one of them following Jefferson upstairs, the others heading for the lounge and kitchen. "Wait!" Mason shouted again, as he tried to get ahead of the officers on the stairs, but the second held him back and Jefferson reached the landing. He glanced at an open bedroom door, and headed inside. Two naked young women were lying in the bed, and one of them sat up and pulled the sheets over them in a flurry of nudity.

"Get dressed!" barked Jefferson, as he slid open the doors of the fitted wardrobes. Mason lurched behind him, and Jefferson turned angrily. "You can get dressed as well!"

"What's this all about?" Mason asked, as the two women slipped out of the bed, grabbed some clothes and headed into the adjoining bedroom to get dressed. The young police officer gasped as they brushed past him, then grinned across the room at Jefferson.

"Nobody in there, Sir," he muttered. Jefferson turned to Mason.

"We're looking for a woman called Phoebe Bartlett, and I have a warrant to search these premises to see if she's here … or has been here recently."

"Phoebe? She's not here. What do you think I was having … a fucking orgy?"

"It looks like you've made a start," Jefferson retorted.

"Look, officer, you've got all of this wrong," Mason muttered quietly, pulling on a pair of shorts and a t-shirt. “I reported Phoebe missing a few weeks ago in Scarborough, so why would I want to hide her here?”

“People do all kinds of strange things, Mr Mason, so we’ve been asked to search here today to make sure that you’ve not been playing silly buggers and hiding Mrs Bartlett here all of the time.”

“Mrs Bartlett?” Mason looked stunned.

“Yes, that’s right, Mrs Phoebe Bartlett, forty-two years old. She’s been missing from her home in Filey since New Year.”

“Jesus Christ,” Mason sat down on the bed, crestfallen. “Look, officer, I was seeing Phoebe at the end of last year, and we arranged to meet again after New Year. I really liked her and we were great together, but when she didn’t get in touch again, I went to Scarborough Police to report her missing. Phoebe married … and forty-two? Are you sure we’re talking about the same woman?” Jefferson reached inside his jacket and brought out a photograph.

“Is this her?”

“Christ, yes, that’s Phoebe.” He fell silent, then looked up at Jefferson. “She’s still missing then? Was she separated from her husband? She certainly acted like a single woman when she was with me.”

“I’m sorry, Mr Mason, but I don’t know the full details of this case. We’re just acting on a request from Scarborough CID to search your premises and to see if there’s any trace of Phoebe Bartlett here.” He paused. “Shall we go downstairs and join the others?" Mason stood up and followed Jefferson downstairs to the lounge, where the two young women were sitting on the sofa and the other officers were watching them. "Any luck?" Jefferson asked the others.

"Nothing, Sir," one of them replied. "We've searched every room, as well as the buildings outside, and there's no trace of her. We've questioned the two young ladies here, and they have nothing to tell us."

"We've never seen her before," one of the women added, glancing at Mason.

"OK then," Jefferson beckoned to the other officers, "I think that's all for now, Mr Mason. Thank you for your co-operation. We're sorry to have disturbed your … activities, but now we can leave you in peace to get on with them."

***

Gary Henderson blinked as he walked out into the bright morning sunlight, lifted his hand to shield his eyes, then glanced along Southall Street, looking for Chris Woodend's car. He spotted it in the distance near Bury New Road, crossed the road and paused, taking a last look at Strangeways, his home for the past five years. Gripping his holdall, he walked down the street to the waiting red car and tapped the driver's window.

"Come on, Wingnut," he grinned, "look lively." He opened the passenger door, slung the holdall onto the back seat and eased alongside Chris Woodend. "Is everything ready, pal?"

"Of course," Woodend nodded, then turned to shake Henderson's hand. "Good to see you back in the land of the living, Gary."

"You too, Chris. Have we far to go?"

"No," he replied, starting the car, "literally a few minutes. Before we set off, Gary, your mother sent you a few things." He gestured towards the back seat. "In the large holdall … clothes mostly … she told me to bin the old one," he added, laughing. "Then there's this," he muttered, passing over a bundle of money, "there's a grand, Gary. It should keep you going until we return to Liverpool!"

"Cheers, Chris."

"Thank your mother. She's been looking after everything while you've been inside."

"OK, I know that there's a lot that needs discussing when I get back home."

"Well, forget about that for now. You've got something else to occupy your time before you have to worry about your business." Woodend eased the car into the traffic on Bury New Road and headed for the city centre. Henderson glanced around at the Boddington's Brewery chimney, the traffic, and the MEN Arena across the road, taking in the normality of the situation.

"Christ, it's good to be free again. You'll never know how much I've missed the everyday things in life … family, a pint with my mates, even going shopping." Woodend laughed.

"Shopping!" he exclaimed, "since when did you

do any shopping?"

"Not often maybe, but it's the freedom to do things that I used to take for granted." He paused in thought. "How are the Reds getting on?"

"Pretty good, Gary, I think they're about third in the table … still a chance of being champions."

"About time, mate, it's been a long time since the glory days. Now, did you say that everything is ready?"

"Yeah, Gary, not too far now," as he turned off the inner ring road, headed along a narrow street near Piccadilly and eased to a halt outside the George Hotel. "Here we are, Gary," he smiled, passing a printed sheet to Henderson, "Room 210. I'll be outside here at 2 o'clock tomorrow afternoon. Have fun!" he added, laughing as Henderson exited the car, reached for the new holdall and walked up the steps to the hotel entrance. He didn't look back as Woodend drove off, and headed for the Reception desk.

"Good morning," he smiled widely at the middle-aged woman behind the desk, "I believe I have a booking?" He passed her the paper.

"Mr Henderson?" He nodded. "Just fill in the details, Sir," she continued, passing him a small sheet and gazing at his deep-blue eyes as he filled it in. "Room 210 is on the second floor, Mr Henderson. If you need any room service, or wish to book a meal … or anything else, please just call me," she muttered, blushing.

"I will, thank you … Gloria," he smiled back, peering at her hotel badge, then he collected the room key and picked up his holdall. "Thanks again," he added, as he headed for the stairs. Henderson had kept fit during his time in prison, and he quickly made his way upstairs without having to catch his breath. He glanced at a brass sign which pointed the way to the hotel bedrooms, then walked briskly along the corridor, turning right and halting outside Room 210. He inserted the key and turned it, pushing open the door and walking into the room. He glanced into the bathroom, then peered around the corner at the king-sized bed in the main room.

"Well, well, a pretty one," gushed a busty brunette who was half-sitting, half-lying on the side of the bed. She looked at Henderson and muttered, "I think it must be my lucky day as well!" She uncrossed her legs and stood up, smoothing down her short skirt, then she moved towards Henderson and placed his holdall alongside the bed. "Let's get comfortable," she spoke softly, smiling widely and reaching for him.

***

Ryan studied the incident board, with its large photo of Phoebe Bartlett and smaller linking photos and information papers. More details had been added since he was last at Northway, and he assessed them mentally while he and the others were waiting for Bentley to turn up for the briefing. It was well past the normal start time, but for some reason the DI had not appeared. Tim Sharpe passed around some fresh drinks; Debbie Chapman and Dennis Slater were studying some notes at Slater's corner desk. Ryan took a gulp of his coffee as Bentley barged into the room, depositing a bundle of papers on the main desk. He looked around the room, then asked: "Where's my drink?"

"Sorry, Sir," Sharpe answered, "I was waiting until you arrived." He headed for the corridor, and returned a couple of minutes later with Bentley's coffee.

"No biscuit?"

"Sorry … were out of them." Bentley grimaced, then sat down and glanced at the top paper. He sipped his coffee, then stood up.

"Apologies for the late start, but I've been waiting to hear from Jefferson at Leeds."

"Jack Mason's house?" Chapman asked.

"Yeah, they visited it this morning, about seven-thirty. Mason let them in, and there were two women in his bed upstairs."

"Lucky bastard!" Sharpe muttered to Slater. "I knew I should have been a footballer."

"What's that, Sharpie?" Bentley asked.

"Oh, nothing, Sir … I just said that I bet Phoebe Bartlett wasn't one of them."

"Hmm, you're right, they were both much younger than her." He looked at the others. "Jefferson found no trace of Phoebe, and he told me that Mason seemed quite shocked to find out that she is married and is much older that he thought."

"He can't have missed her that much, Sir," Chapman commented, "as he's quickly moved on to fresh pastures."

"That's one way of putting it," Sharpe smiled.

"According to Jefferson," Bentley continued, "Mason assumed that Phoebe just didn't want to know, or had found someone else, as he hadn't heard from her for over a month."

"Whatever the truth, I think we can rule out our theory that Phoebe had gone to ground with Jack Mason somewhere," Ryan suggested.

"It looks that way, George, so we're back to the group who last saw Phoebe at the New Year party. How did you get on with Harold Hardy, Dennis?"

"Tim and I caught him just as he was going out to the golf club."

"In this weather, Dennis?" Chapman asked. "Isn't the course waterlogged?"

"I don't know, Debbie, but Hardy told us that he visits the club most days to have some lunch and a drink. Apparently he's the Club Captain this year, so he's expected to show his face pretty often."

"Right. Come to think about it, a friend of mine played a round of golf the other day, so the course must be OK." She paused, sensing the silence and looked back at Bentley.

"What did he have to say, Dennis?" Bentley snapped, giving Chapman a filthy look. "Don't bother with any information about bloody golf!" Bentley was notoriously unfit, and showed little interest in any sport. "Last time we spoke he was pretty insulting about Phoebe, and just slagged her off. Did you get any useful information from him this time?"

"Not much, Sir. He was still hostile about Phoebe, but he did say that Bartlett was getting worried about his wife. She's been away on her own before, but although he's shrugged it off to us, Hardy reckons that Bartlett is very concerned and had expected to hear from Phoebe by now."

"He could be just covering for his friend," Sharpe suggested. "It was difficult for us to judge whether or not he was being genuine." He paused. "I didn't like him, Sir … he's a pompous bugger, if you ask me, and I wouldn't trust him. I think he's glad to see the back of Phoebe."

"How did you get on with Arthur Bartlett, Sir?" Ryan asked.

"Better this time, as Hardy had suggested, Bartlett seemed to be more worried about his wife's disappearance. Isn't that right, Debbie?"

"Perhaps, Sir, he did seem to be more concerned. It was difficult to judge whether that was just a front, but he certainly wasn't as short with us as he had been when George and I interviewed him."

"Yes, but we put him under more pressure, Debbie. He didn't like being surprised at his shop and being questioned by the police in front of his staff and customers. He was clearly anxious to finish the interview quickly, and to get us out of his shop. I'm losing my patience with this case, so I didn't want to piss around with him. We've wasted enough time already looking for this bloody woman, who still might be sunning herself on a beach somewhere with a new bloke." He gulped the rest of his drink. "We still need to have another go at Tom Galbraith, Bartlett's brother-in-law. He and his crew are due back on Tuesday morning, and I want to question all of them before they leave Whitby harbour. George, Tim, you can come with me on that one, and we'll question everybody on that trawler … right?"

"Fine, Sir," Sharpe replied, "as long as the haddock and chips are on you!"

"You'll be lucky, Tim!" Slater joked. Bentley shuffled his notes, then looked at Ryan.

"You've been on your travels, George. How did it go?"

"One or two interesting things, Sir. I spoke to Mrs Archer and she couldn't tell me much more about the Bartletts or the party, but she did let slip something about Frank Parkinson … the farmer. He used to garden for the Bartletts, but she heard whispers that Parkinson was doing a bit more than gardening at *Mandalay*."

"Let me guess," Sharpe interrupted, "he was shagging Phoebe."

"Watch your bloody language, Sharpe," Bentley warned. "Go on, George."

"Tim's right, Sir, that was the rumour Mrs Archer heard, but then someone pinned a joke name on the sign for Parkinson's farm. They changed it from Lamb Rigg Farm to "Limp Prick Farm", and Parkinson stopped gardening soon afterwards." Everyone laughed.

"Christ, that's a good one," muttered Sharpe, wiping the tears from his eyes. "I'll have to remember that one for the lads down at the pub."

"Not yet, you won't, Sharpe!" warned Bentley. "So Mrs Archer suggested that Phoebe and Parkinson had a little fling, which finished after she took the piss out of him?"

"Pretty much, Sir. He stopped doing their gardening soon afterwards, though Mrs Archer told me that the Bartletts had most of their lawns replaced with decking and so on."

"I suppose most of the neighbours would not have been aware that something was going on," Bentley mused, "but Parkinson may have held a grudge against Phoebe."

"But he still was invited to the New Year parties," Chapman reminded them.

"True," Ryan continued, "but Bartlett probably didn't know of the affair, as Parkinson only worked on the garden when Arthur Bartlett was busy with his shops." Bentley looked at him. "That's what Mrs Archer told me."

"This information gives us another angle, Sir," Sharpe suggested. "We already knew that Phoebe had an affair with Jack Mason, now possibly another with Frank Parkinson, so how many more were there?"

"It's good to see that you are thinking straight sometimes, Sharpie," Bentley nodded to him, then he looked across at Ryan. "How about Melissa Jordan, George. Did you find out any more about her?"

"Yes, I did, Sir. I knocked at a few doors opposite her house, and one of her neighbours, a Miss Travers, was very helpful. She's a bit of a nosey parker, and she told me that a middle-aged man has visited Melissa a few times, and that he has a posh green car."

"Arthur Bartlett," Chapman muttered.

"Probably, Debbie. We need to show her photos of Bartlett and his car to confirm that it was him."

"So were they having an affair?" Sharpe's brain was working overtime.

"Not everyone's got sex on their mind all of the time, Sharpie," Chapman snapped at him, "his calls may have been quite innocent … you know, checking to see if Melissa had heard from her sister."

"Yeah, right," Sharpe replied sarcastically, "he could have just phoned to find that out. Let's put two and two together. He's lonely, worried about his wife, and she doesn't like Phoebe, but she's jealous of her wealth and her man. Bingo!" He paused. "The only thing against what I've said is that Phoebe's gorgeous, and her sister is a plump old maid, but who knows … any port in a storm."

"Thank you for your usual eloquence and charm, Sharpie," Bentley smiled, "but we may have something here."

"True, Boss," Chapman continued, "it goes beyond a number of people who simply dislike Phoebe to a number of people who may have a strong grudge against her …"

"… or a reason for wanting her dead," Bentley completed her train of thought. He glanced down at his papers for a moment, then at the incident board. "Somebody must know something," he stated loudly, "so it's time that we put more pressure on these people. Debbie, first thing in the morning we'll arrest Arthur Bartlett and bring him here for questioning. We'll use one of the patrol cars and get there before eight in the morning. Let's make sure that all of his neighbours see us making the arrest. Tim, George, an early start for you. Take another car and drive to Osmotherley, then take Melissa Jordan in for questioning at Thirsk Police Station. I'll clear it for you."

"Batman and Robin, eh?" Debbie Chapman sniggered, as Sharpe glared at Ryan.

"No messing around this time," Bentley barked. "Let's make sure that we get the bastards talking!"

CHAPTER SIXTEEN

The skies were streaked with grey and a bitter easterly wind was blowing as the patrol car neared the cluster of houses around *Mandalay*. "Give the siren a quick blast, Gregson!" Bentley instructed the driver. "Let's make sure that everyone is up!" He glanced round at Debbie Chapman. "Ready?" She nodded, and fastened her coat. Gregson eased the car alongside Bartlett's driveway, and the three police officers got out. Chapman could see Mrs Bond at the front door of her house, and the two Archer children had come onto their driveway to find out what the noise was all about. Bentley pressed the intercom button as Mrs Archer came outside and ushered her children back into the house. She paused at her front door for a minute or so.

Bartlett answered the call. "Mr Bartlett," Bentley barked to the intercom, "North Yorkshire Police. We need to come inside the speak to you. Please open the door." The intercom buzzed, and Bentley pushed open the gate. Another neighbour had appeared at their front door. The three officers walked slowly to Bartlett's house and halted as he appeared. "Mr Bartlett," Bentley spoke clearly, "I want you to accompany us to Scarborough Police Headquarters to answer some questions."

"I spoke to you a couple of days ago, DI Bentley. I have nothing else to add."

"I would prefer it if you just co-operated quietly with us, Mr Bartlett. I don't want to arrest you and make a fuss in front of your neighbours, but I will do so if you don't get ready quickly."

"I'm going to phone my solicitor," Bartlett announced.

"Fine," Bentley replied, "just tell him to meet us at Northway in about half an hour. We'll wait inside until you're ready." They stepped inside into the hallway and closed the door.

Fifty miles away in Osmotherley, Sharpe and Ryan escorted Melissa Jordan to their car before driving her to Thirsk for questioning.

***

Bentley switched on the recording machine and looked across the table. Bartlett had been joined by his solicitor, Jacob Riley, who was almost a double … similar age, similar suit, similar hair style. "It is 9:20am on Saturday twenty-seventh of January, Northway Police Station, DI Bentley and DS Chapman interviewing Arthur Bartlett in the presence of his solicitor Jacob Riley."

"Before we begin, DI Bentley," Riley spoke slowly

with a clipped accent, "have you charged my client with any particular offence?"

"No, I haven't."

"In that case, I would ask you to cease this interview immediately, as my client has made it perfectly clear to you that he has nothing to add to the information he has already provided."

"In the light of new information received, Mr Riley, I can charge Mr Bartlett if you wish, but I would prefer for him to answer some questions voluntarily at this stage." Riley blinked, then whispered in Bartlett's ear."

"I sill feel, that this is a waste of time, DI Bentley, but please continue and get this over as quickly as possible. My client has a business to run."

"He does at the moment," Bentley replied sarcastically. "Mr Bartlett, as you know, we are continuing to make thorough enquiries to try to locate your wife … even though you don't seem too concerned about her disappearance. When I first spoke to you after she had been reported as being missing, you told me that she often spent days or weeks away from home. Is that correct?"

"Yes, I think I told you that she is a free spirit, and that given the age difference between us, I am quite happy for her to spend some time with friends or on holiday."

"Were you not concerned that she may be spending some of this time with male friends, or in other words, having affairs?"

"I love my wife, and trust her fully. She has not given me any cause to suspect her of having an affair."

"Come on, Mr Bartlett, you can't be that gullible? An attractive woman, much younger than yourself, with time and money to do as she pleases ... you can't tell me that you think that your wife is just doing a bit of shopping at Safeway and feeding the pigeons in the park!" Bartlett remained silent. "What's that saying? *There's no fool like an old fool.* Have you heard that before, Mr Bartlett?" Bentley's voice was getting louder. "Your wife was reported missing by a man who'd been screwing her for months!" Chapman glanced at Bentley who was red-faced and breathing heavily. He sat back in his chair and waited for Bartlett to respond. They all looked at Bartlett, until finally he spoke in a quiet voice.

"And he won't have been the first, Detective Inspector. Is that what you wanted to say as well?" Bentley stayed silent. "As you said before, I can't be that gullible, and I'm certainly not a fool." He paused, then continued. "But I am a realist, and I'd rather have Phoebe in my life than not at all, so let's leave it that. I don't want to hear any more about my wife's private life." Bentley sat up.

"It's not that simple, Mr Bartlett. Your wife has been missing for at least three weeks, and you don't appear to be concerned at all. In fact, nobody in your circle of family and friends seems bothered about it, but someone must know something. She can't have disappeared into thin air, and I've been a policeman far too long to think that she's just going to turn up with a deep suntan and a straw donkey! What is your relationship with Melissa Jordan?"

"Melissa is my sister-in-law."

"When did you last see her?"

"She was at the New Year party. Phoebe phones her occasionally, and we sometimes see her when she comes shopping in Scarborough."

"I have reason to believe that you see her more often that that, Mr Bartlett." Bartlett looked at his lawyer. "Have you visited Melissa Jordan at her home in Osmotherley this year?"

"I might have done."

"I know you have, Mr Bartlett. Why?"

"I wanted to know if she had heard from Phoebe."

"Is your telephone not working?"

"I prefer to speak to her face to face."

"Perhaps that's not all that you've been doing face to face."

"What do you mean?" Bartlett asked angrily.

"Look, Mr Bartlett, as you stated before, you are not a fool. Neither am I. We have evidence to suggest that you have visited Melissa Jordan several times recently. Are you having an affair with her?" Jacob Riley touched Bartlett's arm, then whispered in his ear.

"No comment," Bartlett said quietly.

"I ask you again, Mr Bartlett, are you having an affair with Melissa Jordan?"

"No comment."

"Look, Mr Bartlett," Bentley continued more softly, "no-one would blame you if you are having an affair, especially if you think that your wife has been unfaithful to you. You've looked for some love and comfort from a woman that you know, a woman who is close to you. Most people would understand that reaction, Mr Bartlett, but I've got a nasty, suspicious mind. I wonder what's in it for Melissa Jordan? Does she envy her sister's lifestyle so much that she's prepared to do anything, by herself or with somebody else, to take it? Something like murder, Mr Bartlett. Have you and Melissa Jordan murdered your wife and disposed of her car?" Bartlett was red-faced again.

"Really, Detective Inspector Bentley," Riley interrupted, smiling, "have you been watching too many detective dramas on television? What a ridiculous accusation! Do you have any evidence to support your statement?" Silence. "Are you going to charge my client with any offence?"

"At this stage, no."

"Well, I think we're finished here, Detective Inspector Bentley, unless you have some more wild theories that you wish to share with us?"

"No, you can go. Interview closed at ten o'clock." He switched off the machine, as Bartlett and Riley stood up to leave. "This isn't the end of this matter, Mr Bartlett, it's just the beginning." He and Chapman stood up and watched as Bartlett, visibly shaken, left the room.

"Well, that's put the cat among the pigeons," she smiled at Bentley and gathered up her papers.

***

Chris Woodend stood with his back to the wall near the George Hotel, and glanced at his watch again. Twenty-past-two. *Where the hell is he?* He walked a few paces along the street, then turned just as Gary Henderson exited the hotel, gripping his holdall, with a tall, slim blonde-haired young woman clinging to his left arm. They kissed, then she walked down the street past Woodend, turned and waved, then headed for Piccadilly. Woodend waited for Henderson to join him, then asked: "Christ, for a moment I thought that was Fiona Charlton! Who the fuck was she, Gary? What happened to the woman I paid for?"

"Questions! Questions! You're full of them, Wingnut! As for that tub of lard you left for me, well, she only lasted a couple of hours, then fell asleep. She had a big pair of tits, but no staying power. I soon got rid of her!" He nudged his friend. "I thought you knew me better than that. I always preferred blondes."

"Well, yeah, but I thought after five years banged up, you wouldn't be too fussy."

"You thought wrong, Gary. After I tipped her out, I had a quick shower, headed into Chinatown for a meal, then went for a drink and met Monika. She's a Polish student at Manchester University. Lovely girl, Gary." They started walking to where Woodend had left his car. "She left me her number, and under normal circumstances I'd keep in touch, but as you know, I've got unfinished business to attend to." They reached Woodend's car. "Is everything arranged back home?"

"They're all waiting for you in Liverpool, Gary."

"Good! There should be no hitches this time, as my mother's organised everything!" He opened the back door, threw his holdall onto the seat, then settled down for a nap as Woodend started the car and drove off.

CHAPTER SEVENTEEN

George Ryan stood with his arm around Fiona Charlton as the congregation filtered slowly out of Durham Cathedral. "Shouldn't be much longer, Fi, then we can have a look around and have a coffee." A few more stragglers appeared.

"You know, you're full of surprises, George. It was lovely to be able to spend some quality time together last night, the B&B was nice, and now …" she gazed around at the massive columns of the Norman cathedral "… have you some secret plan to woo me by showing me around all of the famous cities and cathedrals of northern England?" They both laughed.

"You've rumbled me, Fiona," Ryan continued, smiling. "Seriously though, I thought it would be nice just to get away for a couple of days. We haven't been able to see much of each other recently, and I have a feeling that I'm going to be really busy next week."

"The missing woman?"

"Yes, something's definitely happened to her, but everyone involved is staying tight-lipped. I think we're going to break the case soon, as we're finding out little bits of evidence, piece by piece, and somebody's going to crack." He turned around and suddenly kissed her. "It's quite exciting, Fi, like sitting on the edge of a volcano before it erupts." He smiled and kissed her again, and saw that the worshippers had gone. He took her hand and guided her towards the great north doorway. "Now I'm going to show you some great knockers!" Fiona looked shocked as George, laughing, eased her along the path.

***

Later that Sunday afternoon, George and Fiona were finishing a meal in a restaurant by the river. She placed her knife and fork on the plate, reached for her glass and sat back. "That was delicious, George, thanks very much … and thanks for a lovely break. Even the church was interesting … I think you've got me hooked … and that joke of yours about those huge door-knockers at the Cathedral," she started giggling, "that still creases me." And no mention of Gary Henderson being released – very thoughtful. They smiled at each other across the table. "What were you saying earlier about a busy week? Debbie says very little about work."

"I can't say too much, Fi, but we've put more pressure on the husband, and it's possible that he was having an affair with his sister-in-law."

“The plot thickens.”

“True, it just opens a few more options. Leeds CID raided that footballer’s house last week and found no trace of the missing woman, so that rules him out of the picture, but it does leave a few family members who really disliked her.”

“Enough to kill her?”

“It’s been done before, so I’m sure that Bentley will keep the pressure on this week. We’ve shaken the tree, so let’s hope that an apple falls to the ground. There’ll be more interviews and searches, and hopefully we’ll get some answers.” He smiled, as Fiona adjusted her blonde hair. “We’ve had a busy bay, but you still look stunning!”

“Well thank you, Mr Romantic.”

“One last drink before we head back?” He stood up and made his way to the bar.

CHAPTER EIGHTEEN

Bentley was in early, studying the incident board as the rest of the team appeared for the morning briefing. He drummed his fingers on his desk as he waited for the team to settle down. Ryan glanced at him, then looked away. Not a jelly-baby in sight – Bentley means business!

"I hope you all had a relaxing day yesterday, because we're going to be busy this week!" he barked. "Tomorrow, bright and early, Tim and Dennis, you're coming with me to Whitby. We'll catch Galbraith and his crew before they leave the harbourside. I want to question Galbraith at the police station, so that his crew won't be under any pressure when we speak to them. Then we can question his missus before he gets home." He glanced towards Chapman's desk. "Debbie, I want you and George to lead a search team at Parkinson's farm. You said that there were a number of old barns on the farm, didn't you?"

"That's right, Sir," Chapman replied. "Parkinson

told us that he rented the land to a neighbouring farm, but he said nothing about the barns."

"I think I remember seeing that they were padlocked," Ryan added.

"Good, then we'll see what he's got inside them," Bentley muttered, smiling. "Who knows, he might have Phoebe Bartlett's Mini hidden in there? You need to sort out a search warrant today, Debbie, … OK?" He turned around to study the incident board again. "Now, last Saturday's interviews. You've had a day or so to reflect on them, so what's the verdict?"

"When George and I first spoke to Bartlett," Chapman responded, "I remarked that he was a very cool customer, and he continued to be at the start of our interview, but when the Boss told him that we knew about some of Phoebe's affairs, he was visibly shaken … not upset, but definitely shaken."

"You're right, Debbie. That clever solicitor knew that we didn't have any hard evidence, but I could tell that Bartlett knows something. He's such a cold fish, but he was wobbling at the end of the interview. If that bloody Riley hadn't stepped in," he grimaced, reddening again, "I think Bartlett would have cracked. I'd have liked to rough him up a bit, just as we did in the old days. That would have saved a lot of pissing about, eh Debbie?"

"Maybe, Sir, and at one point I thought you were going to go for his jugular!" The others laughed as Bentley just shrugged.

"How did it go with Melissa Jordan, Tim? I hope

you and George didn't just eat lots of gingerbread and have a cosy chat."

"Far from it, Sir," Sharpe replied. "I think she was genuinely shocked and distressed when we took to Thirsk for questioning. In front of her neighbours too. She cried most of the way to the station, and hardly stopped when we were there. She denied having an affair with Bartlett, didn't she, George?"

"True, Sharpie, but I felt she was acting out a part. I can see the argument that she and Bartlett were just consoling each other after Phoebe's disappearance, but they've had plenty of time to concoct a story together, haven't they?" He looked at Bentley. "You called Bartlett a cold fish, and I felt that underneath, Melissa Jordan is just the same. Neither of them has shown any real emotion over Phoebe's disappearance. I expected Melissa to demonstrate either love or hate, but, between the sobs, there was nothing. She likes to be seen as the friendly, gingerbread-making old maid who is very popular in the village, but I sense that there's a darker side to her." Bentley thought for a moment.

"Right, get the reports written up today, and Debbie, don't forget to get that warrant. Dennis, can you check out the phone activity between Bartlett and his family and friends from the weekend? Let's see if our interviews with Bartlett and the Jordan woman created any ripples."

***

Gary Henderson studied the papers again, then looked across the coffee table at his mother. "You've done well, Mam. Thanks for looking after everything while I've been occupied elsewhere."

"Occupied elsewhere? That's one way of putting it. I know one thing for certain, Gary. You better hadn't find yourself occupied elsewhere ever again. I've worked very hard to make sure that you won't ever need to turn to crime again." Henderson sipped his tea, then studied the papers again. "It's also cost a lot of money to set everything up, and to protect your identity. You haven't got a lot of cash left now, but I think it's been invested well. I've tried to make sure that all of your eggs are not in one basket. You'll have to work hard to protect all of your investments, and to stay well away from drugs. You've got to draw a line, Gary, and be a respectable businessman." She took hold of his hand, and looked deadly serious. "This is your one chance, son."

"You said that I don't have a lot of cash now, but I still have my house in Crosby, don't I? I can sell it, if need be."

"You need that house, Gary. Don't forget, you have to register regularly with the police for the next three years or so, and maintaining a house here gives you cover. The properties in Spain are your future, but not your present. Don't worry, they're being well looked after by people you can trust, and everything is registered in an offshore company that the police won't be able to trace back to you. As I said before, they should be a good investment, and you'll be legit for the rest of your life." Henderson studied one of the sheets again.

"The villa looks great. I wish we were there now, away from this shitty weather, but you're right, Mam … I must be patient."

"I know it's frustrating, Gary, but you have to be patient. I'll travel to Spain from time to time to make sure that everything is running smoothly. It's costing us at the moment, but once the block of apartments has been built, the rents will build your money up again. We've got trusted people running the bar and shops, so there's nothing to worry about, Gary. I can always send Wingnut out to Spain to supervise everything if you feel we need an extra pair of eyes."

"Wingnut stays with me."

CHAPTER NINETEEN

Tim Sharpe backed himself into a doorway, glanced up at the faint outline of St Hilda's Abbey through the morning mist, and shivered as the rain continued to sweep across Whitby harbour.

"Christ, it's syling down today," a passing fisherman grinned at the three officers as he brushed past them.

"Syling down, what the hell's that?" Sharpe muttered, as he moved his arms up and down his body for warmth.

"Just look out there, Sharpie," Slater rasped, "it's polite Yorkshire slang for saying pissing down." He glanced at Sharpe, who continued to writhe around. "What's the matter with you, you wimp."

"I'm tired, and bloody freezing with all of this waiting around."

"You should have been in the army, Sharpie," Bentley added gruffly, "they soon sort out lightweights like you." He peered along the fish quay, where four fishermen were walking towards them. "Here we go." He moved away from the doorway. "Mr Galbraith," he spoke loudly, holding out his warrant card. "DI Bentley, I need to have a word with you down at the police station." Sharpe and Slater moved to speak to the others.

"Can't we talk here, Inspector, it's been a long trip, and I want to get home?"

"I won't take up too much of your time, Mr Galbraith, but I have a few things to discuss in private."

"Are you arresting me?"

"No, as I said before, I just need a quick word."

"I think I need to call a solicitor."

"That's up to you, but it will only delay things a lot more." Galbraith looked at his crew, then turned back to Bentley.

"Alright, let's get this over and done with."

"Dennis, you can come with me. I'll see you later, Sharpie."

***

"Why are you questioning me again, Inspector? My wife and I have already been interviewed by your team, so what do you expect of me?" The burly fisherman appeared to be quite relaxed.

"As you know, Mr Galbraith, Mrs Bartlett has been missing for some time now, so we're double-checking all of our information, as well as examining fresh angles, and re-interviewing all of the people who last saw Phoebe Bartlett at New Year. One of my officers will speak to your wife again after he has spoken to your crewmen."

"My crew! What can they possibly tell you?" Galbraith gripped the table.

"Well," Bentley continued calmly, "if I remember rightly, two of your crew assisted with the fireworks display and they may be able to provide us with some useful information about Mrs Bartlett's last known movements. As I said before, we're looking at some fresh angles." He glanced down at Galbraith's hands. "If I were you, Mr Galbraith, I would relax and just co-operate with us, then you'll be free to return home to spend some time with your wife." He smiled and waited for Galbraith to sit back in his seat.

"My wife will be worried if I'm late, so please get on with it."

"How would you describe the relationship between Mr Bartlett and his wife?"

"Superficial."

"What do you mean by that?"

"Anyone can see that they're a mis-match. He's nearly old enough to be her father, and she's a good-looking woman. The marriage has only lasted because he's rich, and because we managed to persuade him to make her sign a pre-nuptial agreement when they got married."

"Who do you mean by we?"

"The family, in particular my wife, who is his

sister, and his closest friends."

"Do you think Mrs Bartlett has been unfaithful to her husband?"

"She's got to have been! Come on," he looked at the two police officers across the table, "we're all men of the world here. She's bound to have been screwing around for years."

"Have you any evidence for this accusation?"

"I can't give you any names, but she's always going away on her own … then there was that article in the Scarborough Evening News. We were certain that it was Phoebe getting into that footballer's car."

"Do you think Mr Bartlett knew that his wife had been unfaithful?"

"He never said as much, but he's an old fool … just buried his head in the sand, and always welcomed her back with open arms."

"What would you say if I told you that Arthur Bartlett has been having an affair?" Galbraith laughed.

"Arthur … having an affair … you're bloody joking, aren't you? I think he knows that Phoebe has been playing around for years, but for some reason, he's always prepared to forgive and forget. More fool him, I say."

"Well, Mr Galbraith, DC Slater and I … we operate in the real world, and we know from past experience that if enough people distrust or hate a particular person so much, then eventually, something nasty is going to happen to that person. We have a list of people who had a motive for wanting rid of Phoebe Bartlett, and your name is on it, Mr Galbraith."

"You're way off the mark, Inspector!" Galbraith shouted at Bentley. "I won't say another word until my solicitor is present." He sat back with his arms folded.

"When we've spoken to your wife and other members of the family, Mr Galbraith, I can assure you that it's quite likely that you will need a solicitor!" Bentley's mobile buzzed. He glanced at Slater. "I need to take this," he muttered, then spoke towards the recording machine. "DI Bentley leaving the room at nine thirty-five." He exited the room, leaving Galbraith glaring at Slater. A few minutes later, he returned. "DI Bentley returning to the interview room at nine-forty." He spoke quietly to Slater. "I need a quick word outside, DC Slater." They both stood up and Bentley opened the door and beckoned a constable to come in and keep watch on Galbraith. "Interview suspended. DI Bentley and DC Slater leaving the room at nine forty-two. Constable Bond in attendance with Mr Galbraith." They left the room and Bentley walked a few paces along the corridor, followed by Slater.

"That was Debbie, Dennis. She, Ryan and the search team are at Parkinson's farm. They've found some cannabis."

"I expect Parkinson uses it to ease his mother's pain."

"Don't be daft, Dennis, they've found enough

fucking cannabis to dope all of Scarborough!" Slater was taken aback. "Get on the blower to Sharpe, Dennis. Tell him to get here *asap*, then we're going to Filey. I'll go and get rid of Galbraith, then inform York HQ."

***

Bentley slowed as the car entered the rough lane leading to Lamb Rigg Farm. He swore as he tried desperately to avoid the many potholes which scarred the rough road, and the car bounced gently as he dipped into one of them. "Fucking road!" he exclaimed, as he swerved to avoid another. He braked and crawled along the last stretch until they could see the farm buildings ahead of them. Chapman's car and a large police van were already parked near the farmhouse. Bentley eased his Mondeo to a halt next to the van, and the three officers got out.

"There's the bastard!" Sharpe pointed to Parkinson, who was sitting, handcuffed, in the back of the van. Bentley spotted Ryan in the doorway of the nearest barn, and they headed over to him.

"What have we got then, George?" Bentley called.

"Come and have a look, Sir, you won't believe it." He stood aside as Bentley and the others entered the barn.

"Jesus Christ," Sharpe gasped, "it's like Kew Gardens!" Ahead of him was row after row of large, black pots with green plants in various stages of growth. "What a stink!" Strings of powerful lamps were suspended over the plants, and large floor fans were sited in each section. Bentley could see one of the search team at the far end of the barn.

"This isn't all, Sir," Ryan continued, "come over here." He led them to some stairs, and they climbed up to view another level with row after row of cannabis plants, just like soldiers on parade.

"Bloody Hell!" Bentley muttered, "there must be thousands of the sodding things." He turned to Ryan. "Where's Debbie?"

"She's in one of the other barns, Sir."

"More plants?" Ryan nodded. "Let's have a look." Ryan led the way down the stairs and across the yard to another large building. Bentley noticed that the padlock had been forced open. This barn had two levels of plants, and a large air duct for ventilation. Debbie Chapman spotted the group at the door, and she walked over to join them.

"It's quite a sight, eh Sir?"

"It is if you're a bloody junkie," Bentley spluttered. "It reminds me of a science fiction film I saw years ago," he mused, "*The Day of the Triffids*, I think it was called."

"John Wyndham, Sir," Ryan added. Bentley raised his eyebrows. "He wrote the book, Sir." Sharpe shook his head and looked at Bentley.

"What now, Sir?" he asked.

"I've contacted HQ at York, so they're sending a team to clear this lot." He turned to Debbie. "Forget the flower show … have you found any traces of Phoebe Bartlett?"

"Not yet, Sir. We haven't searched everywhere yet, but there are no obvious signs of any recent digging."

"No Mini?"

"Not in these barns, Sir, there's no room!" The others sniggered. "There are a few smaller buildings that still need to be checked, as well as the fields, though Parkinson told us that he rents them to another farm."

"That's right, Sir, Park Farm, just a few miles away," Ryan added.

"OK, the fields will have to wait for another day, but get in touch with that other farmer, George, to make sure that he does rent them. In the meantime, we can get on with searching these other buildings and the farmhouse, then we can leave the forensic people to sniff around."

"Not too much, I hope," Sharpe muttered, "with all of this cannabis about!"

"For once, Sharpie," Bentley smiled, "that was quite funny."

***

An hour and a half later, the team gathered together again to assess their latest search. "No more cannabis, and still no trace of Phoebe," Bentley concluded.

"Yes," Slater continued, "it's pretty clear that Parkinson used these smaller buildings for his personal use – storing machinery, spare furniture and household items, that kind of thing."

"Years ago, one of them would have been the farm

abattoir," Ryan added, "but now I think he just uses that shed near the lane." He pointed across the farmyard. "That's a solid table in there."

"He obviously didn't want to risk using the farmhouse for any of his other activities," Sharpe muttered. "His mother was probably more with it in the past."

"Hmm, true," Bentley agreed. "Well folks, I think we're done here for today. Parkinson will be remanded in custody, so Debbie, can you arrange some accommodation for his mother, please? I don't think she's fit to look after herself." The others nodded. "The squad from York will take care of the cannabis farm, until it's been completely cleared. And before you ask, Sharpie, no – they don't need a hand. Get back home to your little girl." He looked at the others. "I'm knackered, it's been a busy day. We'll get our heads together in the morning."

CHAPTER TWENTY

"Any thoughts on the Galbraiths?" Bentley yawned as he started the morning summary.

"Mrs Galbraith was pretty tight-lipped," Sharpe said. "She seemed nervous to me, and certainly didn't like being asked questions when her husband wasn't with her. She did admit that she disapproved of Phoebe Bartlett, and had advised her brother not to marry her, but she stated that she hardly spoke to her at the New Year party. When I pressed her further, she just said: "Ask Tom." After that, you called me, Sir, and mentioned the cannabis farm, so I left to join you at the station."

"Galbraith wasn't very helpful," Bentley continued, "in fact he was pretty hostile. He was pretty non-committal at first."

"His mood changed when you suggested that the Bartletts were having affairs, Sir," Slater reminded him.

"True, then he got a bit jumpier when I told him

that if Phoebe has been murdered, he's one of the possible suspects. That's when he clammed up, and asked for a solicitor. We had to leave immediately after that to go to the farm at Filey." He paused. "Any news about the phone activity, Dennis?"

"I'll check now, Sir … let you know in about an hour."

"OK, we'll leave it for now. Oh, just a minute, I almost forgot. Tim, did you have any luck with Galbraith's crew?"

"Not really, Sir. They all said nice things about him, and were obviously loyal to him, said he was a good skipper. Two of them had been at the party, helping with the fireworks, but they left soon afterwards and didn't have anything to say about Phoebe. I gave them my card, just in case one of them remembered something that might be helpful."

"OK, Tim, cheers. This cannabis thing is a bloody nuisance, an unwanted diversion," Bentley rasped. "I'm going to contact HQ to see if they can deal with it. I think we're close to a breakthrough with our search for Phoebe Bartlett, and I don't want to waste time trying to track down Parkinson's accomplices. We just haven't got the manpower here. Bring me a coffee, someone."

***

"I've completed a check on the phone log of Arthur Bartlett and Melissa Jordan following last Saturday, when we brought both of them in for questioning. There's little to report for Melissa," Slater continued, "she phoned Bartlett on Sunday morning, then tried again on Monday and yesterday, but there was no reply. The Galbraiths and Harold Hardy both phoned her on Sunday evening." He paused to give the others time to digest the information. "Bartlett's a bit more interesting. He received the call from Melissa on Sunday morning as I mentioned before, then he phoned his sister and Harold Hardy on Sunday afternoon. Since then … nothing. He hasn't phoned out, and none of the inward calls have been answered." He glanced around the room for reactions.

"Perhaps he's accidentally knocked the phone off the hook?" Chapman suggested.

"Sorry, no he hasn't, Debbie," Slater answered. "There's no engaged tone, and his phone's ringing normally."

"Try phoning him again, Dennis," Bentley instructed, "and George, give Mrs Archer a ring. Find out if she's seen Bartlett in the last couple of days. I'll decide what to do next when you've both got some answers." He looked at Sharpe. "Tim, can you fix us a few drinks while we're waiting?" Sharpe stood up and headed out of the room. "What do you reckon, Debbie?"

"He's probably just refusing to answer his phone, you know, trying to get some peace after the stress of the past week or so." Bentley didn't look convinced. "Whatever the case, we'll know soon enough." Sharpe arrived with the drinks, and passed one to her. "Cheers, Tim." He moved around, giving the mugs to the others. Ryan was conversing quietly at his desk, and when he finished talking, he saw that the others were waiting for him. He nodded to Bentley.

"Right, Dennis, any luck?" Bentley asked.

"Still no answer, Sir. The phone's ringing normally."

"George?"

"Mrs Archer last saw Arthur Bartlett late on Sunday afternoon. Her daughter Amelia spotted him walking past their house. He was wearing a flat cap and a heavy overcoat, and she hasn't seen him since. His car is still on the drive."

"What's going on here?" Bentley muttered angrily. "Is he playing silly buggers with us?"

"He knows we've tracked his phone calls," Slater continued, "so perhaps he's decided to see his friends in person, or even gone to stay with one of them."

"Why no car?"

"I don't know, George. We need to locate him quickly … or to see if, like Parkinson, he's got something to hide at his house. What's the time?" He glanced at his watch. "Debbie, give the magistrates a ring, and tell them that we're coming to collect a search warrant. Dennis, you can hold the fort tomorrow. The rest of you, meet here at eight o'clock tomorrow morning. I'll draft in a couple of constables too. Let's see if the Invisible Man has some secrets hidden in his house. I've always wanted to have a good look around a posh gaff!"

***

"I thought you said that you would be too busy to see me this week?" Fiona asked, sipping her glass of pinot grigio.

"We are very busy, Fi, but I've missed you and wanted a break from the action."

"So I'm just a convenient diversion, am I?" she teased, pouting. George looked shocked, then quickly realised that she was toying with him. "Don't panic, George, I've missed you as well. It's good to pinch a little time together. The paper was full of that cannabis farm at Filey."

"Yes, that took us by surprise. We called the local rag to get them to publish some photos."

"What a find! There must have been thousands of cannabis plants. Have you made any more arrests yet?"

"Not that I know of, Fiona. We've passed the case over to HQ, as we're too tied up with looking for this Bartlett woman. Her husband's gone missing now … hasn't been seen for a few days and he's not answering his phone, so we're raiding his house tomorrow morning."

"The plot continues to thicken! Another busy day for you, George." She glanced towards the bar. "Oh, here's the waitress. We'd better make a choice." They began studying the menu.

CHAPTER TWENTY-ONE

It was raining steadily and the skies were dark and threatening as the two police vehicles drew up outside *Mandalay*. "Try the intercom, George," Bentley instructed, as the others waited inside the car to keep dry. Ryan pulled up his hood, and walked over to the gateway, where he pressed the button. He shook his head, then, as an afterthought, pushed the gate, and it opened. The car and the van drove slowly onto the driveway, then the squad piled out of the vehicles.

"That's the first time it's been open, Sir," Ryan called to Bentley.

"Strange," Bentley muttered, "but let's get on with this. When we get in and de-activate the alarm, do a quick check of all the rooms and the outbuildings to see if Bartlett, or his body, is here. Let me know as soon as you've cleared each area. If he isn't here, we then need to concentrate on finding any evidence to suggest that he's planned to go away for a trip, or to a relative's or friend's house. Check for toiletries and medicines, that kind of thing, and his passport. That shouldn't take too long. After that, in pairs, do a thorough search of every nook and cranny, including the loft and the basement, if there is one." He paused, looking around the group. "Anything else before we begin?" Nothing. "OK, let's get on with it." He led the way to the front door, and gestured for one of the constables to come forward. He was carrying a red door-ram. "Just a minute." Bentley rang the bell, then tried the door handle. It swung open slowly, and he moved inside, followed by most of the others. Two of the constables headed for the outhouses and double-garage. Bentley and Slater began checking the lounge, dining room and kitchen, as the rest of his team headed upstairs.

"Nobody up here, Sir," Sharpe shouted from the landing. One of the constables returned, looking for Bentley.

"Most of the outbuildings and the garage are locked, Sir."

"OK, Grant, have a look in the drawers in the lounge and the kitchen, and see if there's a key-rack on a wall somewhere. If you can't find anything quickly, break a window or batter the door down." Grant nodded, and headed for the kitchen, as Ryan came down the stairs.

"I found this in the bathroom cabinet, Sir."

"What is it?"

"It's a pill-box, Sir, and it has a compartment for each day of the week. My mother has a similar one.

You can see that the pills for Sunday morning have been taken out, but nothing after that."

"Right, George, leave that with me, then see what else you can find." Grant appeared, holding two bunches of keys.

"I found these in the top drawer in the kitchen, Sir. These are the car keys, but I'll see if the others fit the locks in the outbuildings."

"Good." Bentley continued his search in the lounge, and the house was quiet for a while. Grant returned after about ten minutes.

"No trace of Bartlett outside, Sir. We've checked the outhouses and the garage, as well as the garden sheds. Nothing so far."

"OK, Grant, keep at it … every nook and cranny, remember." Bentley rummaged around in the kitchen cupboards, then checked through the cabinets in the dining room. He slid open the door to the conservatory, but there was little there apart from a glass dining table and some wicker seating. Heading upstairs, he had a quick word with the others as they were going through the upper rooms.

"Nothing of importance so far, Sir," Debbie Chapman told him, "but we still have to get in the loft. Has anyone been down the basement?"

"Not yet, Debbie. I didn't notice a door downstairs. I'll go and have another look." He moved towards the landing, as Grant shouted up the stairs.

"Sir! You'd better come and have a look at this … in the outhouse." Bentley moved quickly, followed by the rest of the team, and they headed across a wet paved area to a brick outhouse. It was used as a utility room, with a large tumble-dryer, cleaning equipment, and two large chest freezers. The team filed inside slowly, and gazed at the small pile of frozen packages of meats and vegetables and boxed ready-meals on the top of one of the freezers. Grant stood near a large, round package away from the rest, and as the team gathered around to get a better view, they could see that he had forced open the outer layers to reveal the frozen head of Phoebe Bartlett.

• PART THREE •

CHAPTER TWENTY-TWO

Seven-forty in the morning. The daily routine of having breakfast, getting children ready for school and feeding the family pet was noisily disrupted at Osmotherley as two police cars and a police van drove at speed through the village and parked chaotically on the verges outside Melissa Jordan's cottage. Curtains twitched and some villagers opened their front doors as Bentley's team gathered at the front door and he knocked loudly on it.

"Police! Police!" Bentley shouted, "open the door. Police!" There was no immediate response, so he ushered one of the constables forward. He was just about to swing the door-ram as Melissa, in a mauve dressing gown and with unkempt hair, opened it.

"Oh my God, what's happening?" she cried, stepping back inside the cottage.

"Miss Jordan, we are arresting you on suspicion of assisting an offender, and I have a warrant to search these premises. Go and get dressed, please."

He moved inside, followed by some of the team. "Debbie, go upstairs with her. The rest of you, you all have your tasks. Get on with them!" He stood aside as two of the team headed for the back door and garden, and others began searching the various rooms. A few minutes later, Debbie Chapman escorted Melissa down the stairs, then she and Bentley took her to the unmarked car and drove off.

***

"Before I begin this interview, Miss Jordan, I ought to tell you that at this stage you are just assisting us with our enquiries, but that, depending on your responses to my questions, you may be formally charged with an offence." Bentley and Chapman waited for a response. "You are entitled to call for a solicitor if you so wish."

"That won't be necessary, Detective Inspector. As I told you last Saturday, I have nothing to hide." She appeared to be very calm and confident on this occasion.

"You told us when we last spoke that you are not having an affair with Arthur Bartlett. Is that correct?"

"Yes. We have simply consoled each other over the disappearance of my sister, and the constant barrage of questioning that we have had to endure."

"I see. Have you tried to contact Mr Bartlett since our interview with you?" Melissa paused.

"I phoned him on Sunday morning."

"Have you spoken to him or seen him since then?"

"No."

"Have you attempted to phone him or to see him?"

"No."

"Are you sure about that, Melissa?" She shook her head. "You should know that we are able to trace telephone activity." Melissa thought for a moment.

"Just a minute, I've just remembered. I did try to phone him on Monday or Tuesday, but there was no reply."

"Have you tried to see him?"

"No."

"Has he visited you since the weekend?"

"No, he hasn't," Melissa replied angrily. Bentley sat back and studied her for a minute or so.

"Yesterday, Miss Jordan, a police search team visited Mr Bartlett's house and found no trace of him." Melissa bit her lip. "The house was unlocked and his car was there, but he wasn't at home. We have reason to believe that he left his house on Sunday afternoon." Bentley paused, then continued in a stern voice. "Have you been sheltering him since then?"

"No, I haven't," Melissa muttered, partly covering her face. "I swear I haven't seen Arthur since the weekend."

"As we speak, my team are searching your house and garden."

"Honestly, I don't know where he is." Bentley

looked at Chapman, and waited a couple of minutes before continuing with his questioning.

"Yesterday, Miss Jordan, we found no trace of Mr Bartlett, but we did make a discovery at his house." She looked at him, wide-eyed, starting to breathe heavily. "You need to prepare yourself for some bad news, Miss Jordan." She covered her mouth. "Yesterday, hidden in one of Mr Bartlett's freezers, we found the severed head of your sister Phoebe." Melissa vomited violently through her fingers, the sticky mess covering part of the table and dripping onto the floor. Beads of sweat appeared on her forehead, and she jerked forward and slumped to one side. "Debbie!" Bentley exclaimed, as they both stood up and hurried to the other side of the table. He eased Melissa back up in her seat. "Quickly! Fetch her a glass of water, and bring a mop or bucket, or something to clear up this mess." Chapman left the room and called for assistance. She returned a minute or so later with some water, and a constable arrived with a mop and bucket, and some cloths. "Thanks," Bentley muttered, as he stepped outside the room and called a number on his mobile. The others could hear him speaking quietly in the corridor. When he returned about five minutes later, Melissa was mopping her brow with a damp tissue. She still looked very pale.

"Are you alright, Melissa?" Chapman asked. Melissa nodded slowly.

"Can I go to the toilet?"

"Of course." Bentley gestured for Chapman to

follow her. When they settled back in the room, Bentley resumed his questioning. "I'm sorry to have shocked you like that, but you must realise how serious this situation is. This is now a murder enquiry, and we're looking for the person, or persons, who killed your sister. You need to be totally honest with me, Melissa." He paused. "Is that understood?"

"Yes," she muttered in a whisper.

"Have you seen Arthur Bartlett since the weekend?"

"No, I told you the truth before. I last spoke to him on Sunday." She took a sip of water.

"I have spoken to members of my team at your house. They have confirmed that Mr Bartlett is not there, and have not found any evidence to suggest that he has been there. Do you have any idea where he might have gone? Remember, his car is still at his house."

"Have you tried his friend Harold Hardy, or his sister at Whitby?"

"Not yet, Melissa."

"Well, they might know something, or perhaps one of his staff at his shops. You need to ask them as well."

"Can you explain why your sister's head was in the freezer at Bartlett's house?"

"No," she said, shaking her head, "the last time I saw Phoebe was at the New Year party, and she was alive then. She was still asleep when I left the house." Bentley looked at Chapman.

"Anything else, Debbie?" She shook her head.

"OK, interview terminated at 10.42am." Bentley switched off the machine. "We'll take you home now, Melissa. We are not charging you with any offence at this stage, but you must not leave your village. Understand?"

"Yes," she muttered meekly.

"This is a fast-moving investigation, very serious now, and we may have to speak to you again soon. Is that clear?" She nodded. "Are you feeling well enough to travel?"

"Yes, I think I'll be fine."

"We'll be back at Osmotherley shortly, then perhaps you can call a friend or neighbour to sit with you for a while?" They stood up, and Chapman steadied Melissa as they left the room.

***

"We haven't received all of the test results yet, but we can chew over everything that we've got at the moment." Bentley fished around for a jelly-baby, pushed it into his mouth and sucked on it thoughtfully. He looked at the incident board, with its new cluster of photos of Phoebe Bartlett's head and the outhouse, as well as a separate photo of Arthur Bartlett. He brushed his fingers through his thinning hair, then spoke again. "Christ, what a couple of days!"

"Are you OK, Sir?" Chapman spoke quietly to him.

"Yes, I'm fine, Debbie. Now, where to begin? I've

sent out two more search teams, one to Whitby to the Galbraiths', and the other to Filey to Hardy's house. Their main focus is Arthur Bartlett, but I've instructed them to look for any link to Phoebe Bartlett."

"Like another bit of her body, Sir?" Sharpe asked, smiling. Bentley ignored him and continued with his summary.

"Those teams ought to be reporting back soon. Phoebe Bartlett's head is with Angela Collins at the morgue, and again I hope we can have an initial report before we leave today. We now have a murder hunt on our hands, so I've invited some of the press here later this afternoon. They can headline with a "WANTED" article for Arthur Bartlett, and also appeal for any other information which may lead us to the rest of Phoebe's body. The search teams found nothing at Bartlett's house, nor at Osmotherley, but the sooner we can find it, the sooner we will catch our killer, or killers. Bartlett's the key suspect, but I think it unlikely that he worked alone."

"Why not, Sir?" Chapman asked, "after all, her head was found at his house and he may just have disposed of the rest of her body near the spot where she was killed. They could have been out somewhere in his car, had a row which led to her death, then he buried her body … perhaps on the moors."

"I think that's unlikely, Debbie," Ryan continued. "The forensics team found no traces of her blood in Bartlett's car, and didn't he tell us that he has a bad back? I can't see any way that he could have dragged her body any distance to bury it."

"That's right," Sharpe added, "if she was killed in a car, surely it would have been in her car? It's still missing after all." Chapman nodded, then looked at Bentley and winked, having inspired some lively discussion.

"Why cut off her head, and take it home?" Bentley mused. "It must have been easier to bury a whole body, and another thing, would Bartlett have had a decent knife stashed in the car?"

"Or a spade?" said Chapman.

"Some people keep a spade and suchlike in the boot during the winter months," Slater muttered, "you know, just in case they get stuck in the snow."

"Perhaps he wanted to keep her head as a trophy?" Sharpe suggested.

"That's a bit dangerous," Slater smiled, "especially if one of his friends started rooting around for some fish fingers to make a sandwich!" Polite laughter.

"Were there any traces of Phoebe's blood inside the house, Sir?" Ryan asked.

"No, again, forensics drew a blank."

"Well, it seems fairly certain that Phoebe was killed away from the house," Ryan speculated, "but Debbie and I saw footage of her loading her Mini on Bartlett's security camera."

"The footage that was wiped by him?"

"Yes."

"Perhaps it wasn't her at all," Sharpe aimed for the

top of the class, "but someone dressed like her?"

"In which case," Ryan continued, "Bartlett didn't act alone." He paused. "If there were two people, say Bartlett and Melissa Jordan, it would have been easier to murder Phoebe, to dispose of her body, and to stage her departure and get rid of the car." Bentley's phone rang, and the conversation paused as he answered the call. He listened for a minute, nodded slowly, and muttered: "OK, thanks." He looked around the room. "That was the search teams. Nothing at both houses. Right, where were we?"

"A possible two killers," Chapman reminded him.

"Yes, thanks, Debbie. I still can't understand why Bartlett would want to decapitate his wife, and take the risk of storing her head in a freezer at home." He glanced at his watch. "It's getting on, and I need to be downstairs to speak to the press. I also need to go to the loo. Sleep on it, everyone, and we'll talk again in the morning." He stood up, grabbed some sheets of paper, and hurried along the corridor.

***

Bentley sat between the station commander and Debbie Chapman as the invited journalists settled in their seats. He smiled at two or three familiar faces, looked down at his watch, then opened the briefing.

"Thank you for coming along this afternoon, ladies and gentlemen. For the past four weeks, my team based here at Scarborough Police Headquarters have been searching for Mrs Phoebe Bartlett, a resident of Filey, who was reported as being missing just after New Year. Her husband informed us that his wife left their home to go on a visit, or on holiday, on the third of January, and she hasn't been seen since. We have made thorough enquiries in various locations in North Yorkshire, and have searched some properties. On Monday we learned that Mr Arthur Bartlett had not been answering his phone, so we searched his house at Filey. Mr Bartlett was not at home, but we did discover some human remains in one of the outhouses. These have since been identified as belonging to Phoebe Bartlett. We have therefore launched a murder enquiry, and we are anxious to locate the whereabouts of Arthur Bartlett, as well as receiving any information which may assist us in identifying Phoebe Bartlett's killer, or killers, and when and where the murder took place. We have photographs of Arthur Bartlett for you to use in your articles."

"Am I right in assuming that the Arthur Bartlett you want for questioning is the businessman who owns several jewellery shops in the area?" asked one of the local reporters.

"Yes, you are."

"DI Bentley," asked another, "you mentioned that you have discovered some human remains. Have you found Phoebe Bartlett's body?" Bentley looked at the commander.

"No, just part of it." Murmurs and scribblings.

"Which part?"

"I'm not at liberty to tell you at this moment."

"Do you have any other suspects, DI Bentley?"

"We are keeping an open mind, and we will know more when we have located Arthur Bartlett."

"Do you think he has left the country?"

"That's unlikely, as his car is still at his house, and we have found his passport."

"A few weeks ago," said Angela Robertson, a reporter from the *Scarborough Evening News*, "we ran an article on the Scarborough FC striker, Jack Mason, which included a photo of a mystery blonde entering his car. We then had several phone calls suggesting that the blonde woman was Phoebe Bartlett. Do you think that was possible?"

"Her husband told us that she was a free spirit."

"A good motive for murder?"

"We'll know more when we locate Arthur Bartlett." He glanced around, then a journalist from the *Yorkshire Post* spoke up.

"Am I right in thinking that the Bartlett residence is close to that farm where you discovered a cannabis factory?"

"Yes, the farm is just a short distance away."

"Do you think the two crimes are connected?"

"No, not at this stage, and the CID team at Scarborough is concentrating on the search for Arthur Bartlett and the person or persons who killed his wife." He paused. "Are there any more questions about that matter?" Silence. "Thank you for your attention, ladies and gentleman." Bentley watched the journalists disperse.

"That should make some interesting reading in the morning, Don," the commander remarked.

"I guess so, Sir, and it's good timing, as people have more time to read the papers at the weekend. I just hope we get a lead from the coverage, because we need to find Bartlett quickly."

CHAPTER TWENTY-THREE

"Anything new, Sir?" Debbie Chapman asked, anxious to hurry along the briefing as she was going to Leeds for the weekend.

"Not a great deal, Debbie. The papers will be out today and tomorrow, so we'll have lots of headline coverage, and hopefully, one or two new leads from it."

"I've got a copy of the *Whitby Gazette*, Sir," Ryan said, holding up the newspaper, so that the others could see the face of Arthur Bartlett dominating the front page.

HUNT FOR A KILLER!

"Not very imaginative," Slater commented, "but at least it's the main story."

"I'll have a look at that when we're finished, George. I don't want to take up too much of your time, so that can enjoy the rest of the weekend. I'm sure that we're going to have another busy week ahead of us."

"The *Scarborough Evening News* is out later today, Sir," Sharpe continued, and I'll try to get hold of a copy of the *Yorkshire News* as well."

"That's very team-spirited of you, Sharpie," Bentley smiled, "I'm impressed."

"Laura's going away for a girlie night to Newcastle, Sir, and I'm babysitting, so I want all of the reading that I can get."

"I'd offer to help with changing all of those shitty nappies, Tim," Chapman grinned, "but I'm away to Leeds myself. Good luck with them, and don't forget to wash your hands!" Sharpe grimaced at the thought.

"I've had an initial report from Angela Collins," Bentley got the briefing back on track. "She's examined Phoebe's head, and said that it was removed very neatly, not just hacked off. She suggested that it was done by someone who had a little knowledge of these things … who knew what they were doing."

"Don't tell me," Sharpe wise-cracked, "we're looking for someone with surgical knowledge, or a butcher." He pretended to ponder on it. "I know!" he exclaimed, "it must be Jack the Ripper!" They laughed at his theatricals.

"OK, back to reality," Bentley muttered soberly. "Angela also said that Phoebe's pupils looked to be very dilated."

"Poisoned?" suggested Ryan.

"It's possible," Bentley continued, "but we'll have to wait until Angela's run some more tests." He paused. "In fact, we're got a bit of a waiting game now. As I said before, we need to locate Arthur Bartlett as soon as possible. Keep checking the telephone log, Dennis, and next week we may have to check the B & Bs and hotels along the coast to see if he's lying low in one of them. Let's hope that we get some calls from the public when they've read the papers, or even better, a sighting of the bastard. No car, no packed bag, no passport … surely he can't be far away?"

"I was thinking again about his security tape, Sir," Ryan spoke out, "the one that he showed to Debbie and myself. Arthur Bartlett was on that tape, and so was a woman who looked like Phoebe, so if it wasn't her, ought we bring in people like Melissa Jordan or Tom Galbraith for more questioning? In our last briefing, we all thought that Bartlett must have had an accomplice, you know, even just help with the disposal of this wife's body."

"That's probably right, George," Chapman responded, "but we haven't got the tape any more, have we? Bartlett wiped the key section."

"Debbie's right, and I think that anyone we question will flatly deny any involvement. We've no real evidence yet, George, and any decent solicitor would just advise their client to make no comment." Bentley stood up, and checked his watch. "As I said earlier, we're playing a waiting game, so let's see what

Monday brings. Go and enjoy the weekend."

***

Gary Henderson sat back in his seat, and looked across the table at his mother. He took a drink of his lager, and glanced around at the other tables in the pub's restaurant, which was full of couples and families enjoying their Sunday lunch.

"I've been doing a lot of thinking, Mam," he spoke softly to her. "The only things keeping me here are my house in Crosby, and the regular visits I've got to make to the police station. I don't want to fester here waiting for my parole period to end, looking over my shoulder to see if some low-life I've upset in the past is trying to do me over. I don't want to be the victim of a gangland hit like Dad. After all, some of the other drug gangs may view me as a threat, now that I've been released." Janet Henderson continued to listen patiently to her son, his deep-blue eyes sparkling as he outlined his plans to her. "Don't worry, I don't want to be involved in drugs ever again. I've made my money, my fortune, and thanks to you it's been invested wisely in Spain. That's where my future lies, Mam … not here in Liverpool."

"I understand what you're saying, kid, but as I was telling you the other day, there's still a lot of work to do out there. Those apartments haven't been finished, and that's where a lot of your money has been spent."

"Yes, but the flats aren't everything, are they? I've

got the bar and the shops, and the villa's all been paid for, hasn't it?"

"True."

"Well that's settled then. I just need another identity, then I can go over there and supervise everything myself. The police will soon forget about me here."

"You're joking, aren't you? What about Interpol? It's not as easy as it used the be on the Costa del Crime, you know. Someone will recognise you."

"No, they won't. As I said before, I'll have a different identity. I know people who can easily fix that for me."

"A great-looking guy like you … the police will just have to follow the queues of blondes going into your villa!" Henderson laughed.

"I may be good-looking, Mam, but I'm not stupid. No-one will recognise me, I'll have some new people working for me, and I'll make sure that I stay in the background. After all, I'll be legit, won't I, just a harmless businessman?"

"What about the house in Crosby?"

"I'm going to sign it over to you, Mam. You can sell it if you wish, and do what you like with the money. After all, I owe you big-time. I want to leave all of my past here when I go, and make a fresh start out in Spain." He smiled widely.

"And when is all of this going to happen?"

"Soon, Mam. You'll know when I've gone, but it

will be soon." He drained the rest of his drink.

***

Fiona relaxed in George's arms as they lay with their feet up on his sofa. She moved slightly and leaned up to kiss him. "Thanks for tonight, George. I really enjoyed the play. I hadn't realised the theatre could be so interesting, so different. I've never seen a play where the action is on three levels … a bit weird."

"I'm glad you enjoyed it, Fi. I'm not a great theatre-buff myself, but I do like watching the occasional play. We're lucky here in Scarborough having Alan Ayckbourn as the resident playwright. *Things We Do For Love* is his latest play. He's a key figure in contemporary theatre."

"Whatever you say, darling, I'll believe you." She cuddled back into him, and closed her eyes for a couple of minutes. "Hey, what happened to the coffees?"

"Sorry, I was just drifting off then … completely forgot about them. I'll get them sorted, then we can go to bed." He eased himself off the sofa, and headed for the kitchen. Fiona glanced around his flat as she waited for the coffees to appear. George returned a few minutes later carrying two mugs, which he put down on a side table. He looked at Fiona, who was engrossed in a book. "What's that you're reading?"

"Your sketch-book, George." She flicked over another page. "I hadn't realised that you were such a talented artist!"

"I wish. That's the book which belongs to Amelia

Archer," he said, looking at her puzzled expression, "you remember, the deaf mute I told you about." The penny dropped.

"Oh, the little girl who lives next door to the Bartletts?"

"Yes, that's her … she's a great artist for her age."

"Wonderful," Fiona muttered through a mouthful of coffee.

"Don't splutter on that book, Fi," George smiled. "I promised to return it in good condition, and I haven't looked at it properly yet. We've had such a busy week, I'd forgotten about it."

"Her animal sketches are marvellous, George, she's so talented." She paused. "What's this one, George?" He took the book from her and looked at the sketch, flicking back and forth to understand the context.

"Well it's obviously a van, but that could be important in our investigation, Fiona." He sat down next to her. "OK, it's just a van, but can you see that square board behind the van?" Fiona leaned forward.

"Yes, what of it?"

"That looks like the sign for Frank Parkinson's farm. It's just along the lane from her home … and from the Bartlett's house." He flicked through a few more pages. "Look, here's her sketches of the New Year fireworks display at the Bartlett's house. That van must have visited Parkinson's farm before then, and I know that he doesn't have one like it."

"Isn't that the farm where they found all of those

cannabis plants?" George nodded. "Look, George, she's drawn some letters on the side."

"Yes, BEN… and REMOV …, it must be a removals van." He turned to Fiona. "The York team are dealing with this case. I'll have to get a copy of this for them. It may help them to identify one of Parkinson's accomplices." He kissed Fiona. "Well done, we'll make a detective of you yet!" He sipped his coffee. "I'll have to study the rest of this book, Fi. There may be some useful clues for our murder investigation." She took his mug and buried the sketch-book under some papers again.

"You can forget about that book tonight, Sunny-Jim. I've got something else that you need to study!"

CHAPTER TWENTY-FOUR

"The local papers have been inundated with sightings of Arthur Bartlett," Bentley brandished several sheets of paper, "so we'll have to get cracking to see if any of them provide any useful leads for our investigation."

"We'll be chasing our tails all day, Sir," Sharpe complained. "I bet most of them tell us that they've seen him in a jeweller's."

"Don't be so pessimistic, Tim," Chapman scolded him, "this is our best chance of finding him quickly and getting this murder solved."

"Debbie's right," Bentley continued. "If we get just one sighting of Bartlett after Sunday afternoon, this exercise will have been worth it. OK, you can stop moaning and get on with it." He handed the sheets around.

"Have you a minute, Sir?" Ryan asked.

"Sure, what is it, George?"

"I found this in Amelia Archer's sketch-book last

night, Sir," he passed the copy to Bentley. "Actually, Fiona spotted it. I borrowed the book, but haven't had the time to check through it properly," Ryan confessed, as Bentley peered at the sketch.

"Explain, George."

"Amelia's always drawing sketches of anything she sees near her house – animals, people, buildings, that kind of thing. She did several sketches of Phoebe Bartlett, but this drawing seemed out of place, until you realise that that sign behind the van is the wooden sign for Lamb Rigg Farm."

"The cannabis factory, of course. The sign is by the side of the road, isn't it?"

"That's right, Sir, and this white van doesn't belong to Parkinson."

"OK, the lettering ought to identify the owner. I'll send this to HQ, George, and find out how their investigation is going. This may be a new piece of evidence for them." He smiled. "You'll have to give Fiona a pat on the back … it's not often that someone gets ahead of the Boy Wonder!"

"Cheers, Sir," Ryan muttered sheepishly.

"How is she, George?"

"Fine, Sir, we went to see a play last night. She seems quite relaxed at the moment, and Debbie hasn't noticed any anxiety. We haven't seen a lot of each other recently, what with this Bartlett business, and she's often tired after a day's shift, but I hope we can get away for a holiday soon … when this case is over."

"Good man, George, look after her. With any luck, we'll find Bartlett soon, and get this case closed." He smiled. "Then you can look through some brochures!"

"Any more news from Maddie, Sir?"

"Not yet, George, but it's still early days. I wish I had her address or phone number, then I could contact her to say that they're all welcome any time!" Ryan could see that the DI was getting emotional, then he regained his usual composure. "Now, bugger off! You've got work to do!" He picked up the sketch, and studied it again.

***

"Well done, everyone. I think we've got through most of the contacts we've received, so where are we with this?" Bentley looked at each face in turn.

"We put our heads together about half an hour ago, Sir," Chapman spoke first, "just to see if we've got any common ground. There's been quite a few hoax calls, and wild goose chases. One woman even tried to convince us that she saw Bartlett in Aberdeen on Monday." Bentley smiled.

"That's a long way to go to watch a soccer match," he muttered. "OK, Debbie, did you find any plausible leads?"

"Yes, we think so. We've had calls from three unrelated people to say that they saw Bartlett late on Sunday afternoon, either waiting for, or on the bus to Leeds."

"Leeds … why Leeds?" Bentley thought for a

moment. "He hasn't any strong connections with Leeds, has he?"

"That footballer Jack Mason lives there, Sir," Sharpe suggested. "He's the one I interviewed, the one who'd been shagging Phoebe Bartlett. Perhaps Bartlett has found out where he lives, and wants to exact some kind of revenge on him."

"No, you are way off the mark, Sharpie," Debbie Chapman sneered. "Anyway, why trail all the way to Leeds on a bus, when he could have driven there in less than two hours?"

"Someone told us that Arthur Bartlett met Phoebe at a party in Leeds, didn't they?" Ryan asked. "He may have an old friend or two in the area, but there again, he could have got off the bus at any point on the journey."

"That's true, George," Slater continued, "we haven't had a sighting of him leaving the bus as yet."

"He could have been making for Osmotherley, Sir," Ryan added. "He would just have to get off at Malton, where Melissa Jordan might have collected him. Should we check on her again first thing in the morning?"

"I'll ask the lads at Thirsk to pay her a call, but our main priority is interviewing the bus driver," Bentley decided. "With any luck he'll remember where Bartlett got off the bus. We'll check with the depot in the morning." He reached for his coat. "By the way, Angela Collins has confirmed that Phoebe was poisoned, but couldn't be exact about the day she died." He looked at Debbie Chapman. "We're nearly there, folks. We just need one good break, that's all."

"I expect we'll receive some more calls tomorrow, Sir," Slater spoke optimistically. "It usually takes a few days for all of the calls to filter through, sometimes it can be a week or two."

"What, when someone recognises the face in his fish-and-chips paper?" Sharpe laughed.

***

Bentley and Ryan were waiting patiently in the staffroom at the bus depot on Westwood Road. They had spoken to the manager, Mr Gawne, and he confirmed that the driver they needed to see, Bob Thompson, was due in soon for his late morning shift. Bentley's mobile buzzed, and he stood up and moved to a quiet corner to answer it. He returned a few minutes later. "That was Tony Nicholson at Thirsk, Debbie. He and another constable called on Melissa Jordan at Ormotherley, but there was no sign of Bartlett. They checked with that woman across the road, and she hadn't seen him either." He checked his watch. "That driver should be here soon."

"The others will have plenty to do, Sir. I'm sure that a lot more calls will come in today. We'll have to ask the newspapers to keep drip-feeding the story if we don't have a breakthrough soon." She looked up as Mr Gawne appeared with one of the drivers. They walked over to the police duo, who stood up.

“This is Bob Thompson, DI Bentley.” They shook hands. “You can use my office if you wish.”

“Thanks, Mr Gawne.” They walked along the corridor until they reached the office.

“Just shout if you need any more tea or coffee,” Gawne muttered, finding a seat for Debbie Chapman before he left the room. Thompson, a bespectacled middle-aged man looked nervous as he waited for Bentley to speak.

“Don’t worry, Bob,” Bentley smiled, “you haven’t been caught in a speed camera, or anything like that.” Thompson relaxed a little. “We’ve come to see you about a totally different matter.” He paused. “Have you heard about a murder that took place in Filey recently?”

“Yes, the missus mentioned it last night. She said it was in all of the papers, but I was too knackered when I finished my shift, and I forgot to look this morning before I left for work.”

“I’ve got one of the papers here,” Bentley continued, showing him the front-page story in the *Scarborough Evening News*. What we need to know first, Bob, is did this man get on the Leeds bus on Sunday afternoon?” Thompson wiped his glasses on his jumper, then looked at the photo of Bartlett.

“Yes, I remember him, very quiet sort of bloke, sat on the edge of his seat so that no-one could sit next to him. He seemed to have a lot on his mind, took a few minutes to sort out the right money for the fare.” Thompson smiled. “I kept glancing at him through the mirror, but he barely moved, just sat staring in front of him."

"OK, Bob, that's good," Bentley nodded, "but now here's the important question … can you remember where he got off?"

"Oh yes, he didn't travel very far with us. This bloke got off at Malton, then he wandered across the road towards Pickering. It was dark, so I soon lost sight of him."

"Malton!" Chapman exclaimed, "what on earth was he doing there?"

"I can't help you there, love. He just got off the bus, without saying a word, and disappeared into the night."

"Well thanks, Bob," Bentley stood up and gestured for Chapman to follow him, "you've been very helpful." He passed him a card. "If you think of anything else, please …" They left the office.

***

"Right, so we concentrate our search on the Malton area," Bentley looked stern, as he summed up the interview at Scarborough bus depot.

"Shall I contact the local papers, Boss?" Slater asked.

"Please, Dennis. Give them an update on the last sighting of Bartlett at Malton, and get them to ask dog-walkers and hikers to keep their eyes open for a dead body on the moors and farmland around there."

"Do you think he knew where he was heading, Sir?" Ryan continued.

"Judging by the description given by Bob Thompson, my guess that his head was everywhere, he was perhaps very depressed, so he's just got on a bus to Malton, then walked along the road to the moors."

"That's right, Boss," Sharpe was eager to contribute, "it was pitch dark, so he could have wandered anywhere … anywhere, that is, until he's fallen down a bloody hole, or something like that. If his body isn't visible, it could take weeks to find him." He sat back.

"At the moment," Bentley began concluding the briefing, "we've got to rely on Joe Public. We haven't the manpower to organise search parties, and even if we did, where the hell do we begin looking? No, we keep chasing up the sightings until one of them leads us to Bartlett."

***

Wednesday evening. George had arranged to see Fiona after her shift finished at Whitby, and had suggested that they go for a meal to the restaurant where they had enjoyed their first meal together last summer. Fiona had travelled by bus, so that she could leave her car at Scarborough, ready for the following day's commute. The evening had gone well, but the conversation inevitably touched on the hunt for Bartlett.

"We've had a good response from the public, Fi, but the trail's gone cold at Malton. Some of the team are still convinced that Bartlett and Melissa

Jordan are working together, you know, that's she's arranged a safe hiding-place for him somewhere, waiting until the two of them can disappear, but I disagree. The descriptions we have are of a man in turmoil, someone with a lot on his mind, someone with a decision to make. I think that Bartlett was genuinely in love with his wife, and was prepared to let her do anything, as long as she stayed with him and kept up the pretence of a normal marriage. Melissa had a lot to gain if she could convince Bartlett to leave Phoebe and then to pair up with her."

"But you don't think he was interested?"

"No, but he's put up with her trips with a friend in the past, and her mystery holidays, so his erratic behaviour convinces me that this time it's different. I don't think he's the killer, and I'm convinced that he knows who is responsible for her death, but why is he protecting them?" Ryan glanced out of the window, deep in thought.

"Coffee, Sir?" The waitress brought him back to reality.

"Jesus, sorry Fiona, I was miles away. Very rude of me. Would you like a coffee, love?"

"No, thank you," Fiona answered the waitress, then she turned to George. "Come on, Sherlock. I shouldn't have opened my mouth about Phoebe's murder. Let's get back to mine, then we can have a nightcap there. Debbie will be in bed by the time we get back."

***

The team were still chasing leads early the following afternoon. Ryan looked across at Slater, then stood up and moved to his desk. "Dennis, I almost forgot. Can you run a check on this number-plate for me?"

"Sure, George, what's this about?"

"It's just a car that I've noticed parked a few times along the street from Debbie's house. Once or twice, I thought I saw someone sitting in it. It's probably nothing, but can you just put me at ease?"

"Still protective over Fiona, George?" Ryan nodded. "I'll get these other calls sorted out, and let you know when I've got a name. OK?"

"Cheers, Dennis." Ryan returned to his seat, as the DI's phone rang. He listened for a few seconds, then spoke loudly:

"Been found? Where?" He listened again, as the others halted their work and waited for the answer. Bentley nodded and jotted a few words down on his pad, then nodded again. "Thanks, Mike, thanks a lot." He put the phone down and looked around the room.

"Is that Bartlett, Sir," Sharpe asked anxiously. "Have they found his body?"

"No, Sharpie, they've found something else." He paused. "Phoebe Bartlett's right leg."

CHAPTER TWENTY-FIVE

Bentley drove the car as close as possible to the site of the former orchard in the grounds of the old mansion at *Abbotsfield*. It was sleeting now, and dark, but the headlights picked out the yellow and white tape screening off the area, and a yellow-coated constable standing nearby. Bentley slid down his window and had a quick word with him, then he and Sharpe exited the car and moved around to the boot, picked out some waterproofs and made their way through the tangled undergrowth to the forensics awning, which was brightly illuminated. Slater had remained behind at the station, chasing up calls until his shift finished, leaving Chapman and Ryan to visit the dog walker who had made the grim discovery.

Bentley ducked under the tent flap, followed by Tim Sharpe, who headed for a corner where he shook his waterproof. Bentley glared at him, then made his way gingerly to the mound of earth where the discovery had been made. "How are you getting on, Angela?" he asked one of the kneeling figures.

"Not too bad, Sir," she muttered, pointing to an area of the mound where most of the black-wrapped package had been revealed. She stood up, and drew Bentley's attention to the foot, which had been exposed. "Some rats, Sir, or maybe a fox, or both ... they've been having a nibble, but it's pretty clear that the leg belonged to a woman."

"You don't need to be a rocket scientist to work out which woman that was," Sharpe joked softly, having moved behind Bentley to get a better view. Bentley elbowed him to move back, then knelt down to study the package.

"Looks like the same kind of wrapping that we found on her head, Angela. Are you going to be here much longer?"

"I hope not, Sir. It's a foul night, and I'm getting cold," she muttered. "The lads have had a quick look around the area, but they can't do much more until the morning. The package has become frozen into the mound, so we can't remove it quickly."

"I don't envy you your job, Angela," Bentley rasped, warming his hands. "I'll leave a car here when you've done, and then arrange for a search team to have a look tomorrow, but my hunch is that we won't find any more parts of her here, Angela. What do you think, Sharpie?"

"I think you're right, Sir. We now know that Bartlett, or whoever killed her, didn't just decapitate her and bury the body ... no, it looks like he's scattered the poor woman all over north Yorkshire."

"Hmm, could be. Right, we'll leave you to it, Angela, and I'll see you tomorrow afternoon, if that's OK?"

"Fine, Sir. Think of me when you're having a nice warm cocoa back home!" Bentley and Sharpe laughed politely, then made their way back to the car.

***

"We won't keep you long, Mr Askew," Debbie Chapman smiled. "Can you just give us a brief account of what happened today?"

"There's not too much to say, DS Chapman," he replied, as his wife arrived with some mugs of tea.

"Thank you," Ryan said, placing his notepad on his knee.

"I often walk Sheba in the old mansion grounds," the portly Askew began. "She likes it there, because I can usually let her off the lead and she can go off rooting around in the undergrowth. The forecast wasn't good today, so I brought her there a bit earlier than usual, and when she got behind those mounds, she began barking. I generally stick to the path, but she wouldn't come back to my call, so I battled my way through the brambles until I could see that she was barking at some toes poking through some black wrapping."

"Ooh, gives you the creeps," his wife shuddered, stroking the dog. "Poor Sheba." Mr Askew glared at his wife.

"Never mind poor Sheba, Sharon. What about

the poor woman who's been killed?" He turned to Chapman. "I guess the leg belonged to that Bartlett woman in the papers?"

"Most likely," Chapman replied. "Now it's probable that the leg was buried there recently, Mr Askew, so when you've been walking Sheba, have you ever seen anyone acting suspiciously in the area of the grounds?"

"No, I can't say I have."

"Have you seen anybody carrying a spade, or something like that?" Ryan added.

"No, sorry."

"Have you ever seen this man, Mr Askew?" Chapman continued, handing him a photo of Arthur Bartlett. "He's quite tall and thin, late fifties."

"He's the man you're looking for, DS Chapman, isn't he?" Chapman nodded, "but I haven't seen him on the walk. Most people have a dog or two with them, not a spade. I'm sorry I can't be more helpful."

"Every piece of information is helpful to us, Mr Askew, so thank you for your time."

"You're welcome." He thought for a few seconds. "Surely anyone burying the leg would have done it late at night, wouldn't they, so that nobody would see them?"

"Probably, Mr Askew, but some killers are careless. They're not always professionals," Chapman smiled. She stood up, and passed a card to Askew. "Just in case." He nodded, as Ryan stood up, then they said their goodbyes, and left the house.

***

"Did Bartlett act alone?" Bentley selected a red jelly-baby from the paper bag on the table. "What does our latest find tell us?" he added, as he thrust the jelly-baby into his mouth and chewed it enthusiastically.

"Well, we thought it impossible that he could have killed Phoebe, beheaded her, then taken the rest of her body somewhere and buried it. His doctor has confirmed that he has a bad back, and he always moaned about it, so he could not have carried out any physical task like that on his own. Agreed?" Chapman looked around for confirmation. "We now know that Phoebe's body has been cut up into more easily transportable pieces, so perhaps he could have been a lone killer? What do you think?" Bentley watched the others as they prepared to respond.

"If he worked alone," Ryan spoke first, "where did he kill Phoebe and dismember her body? We found no traces of her blood at his home, and I don't think he would have had the stomach to do it. It's one thing to kill someone in a moment of rage or passion, but quite a different thing to calmly cut up someone's body, or in this case his wife's body, into pieces." He glanced at Bentley. "Bartlett must have had an accomplice, Sir."

"That makes sense, George," Sharpe continued, "perhaps he worked with someone who had some experience in cutting up things, such as a farmer or a fisherman."

"Parkinson or Galbraith, do you mean?" Chapman asked.

“Maybe, Debbie,” Sharpe said, thinking things through, “for didn’t we say that Phoebe may have had a fling with Parkinson? If so, why not Galbraith as well? If she spurned them, or humiliated them, either of them could have been a willing accomplice for Bartlett, and well-prepared to do the dirty job of dismembering her body.”

“Stranger things have happened,” Bentley spoke at last, “but if we don’t find Bartlett alive, it’s going to very difficult to find the evidence to implicate someone else. Tomorrow’s papers will headline the latest find, and there’ll be more lurid speculation this weekend, so be prepared for another deluge of calls. Let’s hope that we get a crucial lead this time.” He looked at his watch. “OK, time to go home. I’ll only call you in if there’s a big development, so enjoy the break!” He looked for his coat, and the others prepared to leave.

“Oh, George,” Slater tapped him on his shoulder, “before you go, I’ve got that information you wanted.”

“The car, Dennis, it had slipped my mind with everything that has happened today.”

“Easily done, son. The car belongs to a Christopher Woodend … home address, Toxteth, Liverpool. I’ve done a check on him,” he added, flicking to a page on his computer, “here he is.”

“What big ears!”

“Yes, his nickname is Wingnut. He’s been in a bit of bother over the years, nothing too serious …

breaking and entering, drugs, that kind of thing. He's done a bit of time, but nothing for a few years. There's a note here about one of his known associates, a Gary Henderson, a top man in the Liverpool drug scene. He was released a couple of weeks ago from Strangeways."

"Cheers, Dennis, it's probably nothing, I was just curious, but thanks for taking the time." *For God's sake, don't do any more digging about Henderson, and find the link with Fiona*. "I'm starving! I think it's an Indian for me tonight." He headed for the corridor. "See you, Dennis."

CHAPTER TWENTY-SIX

Fiona Charlton was working the morning shift at Whitby, but George had suggested that they spend the rest of the weekend in County Durham, visiting Beamish Museum on Sunday. "Another museum, George. Are you trying to educate me!" Fiona laughed.

"Listen, Fi, Beamish is different to the others. They call it a museum, but it's a huge site in a valley near Chester-le-Street, and everything is outdoors. They have a recreated pit village, where you can go down a drift mine, an Edwardian town and school, a wartime farmhouse … lots of things, Fi, and you can walk everywhere or travel around on an old tram. It's very authentic, and has won lots of awards."

"OK, George, you've sold it to me. I must admit that it does sound better than a building full of stuffed birds!"

"Honestly, it's nothing like that. I can guarantee that you'll really enjoy it." She smiled, having teased him again. “I’ll collect you after your shift, and I’ll book a nice hotel for Saturday night.” He paused for a few seconds. “There is something else, Fi … my parents live in Darlington, and I wondered if you fancy meeting them, briefly that is, on Saturday afternoon. I saw them at Christmas, and they’re curious about you.” He waited for a response.

“They’re not expecting wedding bells, are they, George?”

“Hell, no, nothing like that. We won’t be there long. I just thought that we might call in as we’re in the area.” He laughed. “There’s no sinister master-plan behind this, honestly!”

“Go on then … I suppose I’ll have to dress smartly for this one?”

“No way, just wear what you would do normally, you know, smart-casual, that’s all you need to do. Are you sure you don’t mind?” She shook her head. “Good, I’ll give them a ring. Oh, and make sure you bring a warm coat tomorrow, Fi. It’ll be pretty cold at Beamish this time of year. Are you sure you’re happy with all of this?”

“Yes, George, make all of the arrangements, and I’ll see you tomorrow. ‘Night.” The phone went dead.

Good, he thought, something to look forward to, and I haven’t mentioned the car in the street. I’ll ask Bentley to contact Liverpool CID, and check Henderson’s movements since being released. If the car appears again, I’ll have to act.

***

"Yesterday was nice," Fiona smiled, as she and George boarded an old tram to take them to the other side of the valley, and the recreated Edwardian town. "Your Mam was really sweet, and it was kind of her to ask us to stay for the night."

"She was being nosey, Fiona, a typical mother. We're not that close, and I don't see my family very often, so I expected her to make a big fuss. At least my parents have met you now, and I think they approved."

"Well I tried my best," Fiona smiled and kissed George on his cheek. "Thanks for last night too. The hotel was lovely, and you're becoming quite a Romeo." George blushed, and glanced out of the window.

"Almost there," he muttered, changing the subject. "It's a beautiful sunny winter's day, but make sure that fasten your coat … and wear a hat."

"I look stupid," she said, tucking her long blonde hair into her coat, then examining the large pom-pom on her woolly hat. "These woolly hats are for children!"

"Wear the hat!"

"Yes, Sir!"

***

The bright sunshine had softened the frosty fields by lunchtime, and Amanda Sutcliffe and Mary Dawson, two twelve-year-old friends from Malton, had just finished their meal and were putting on their thick jackets, ready to spend some time with Amanda's two horses in the paddock behind her parents' detached country home.

"We're going to give Saracen and Prince a gentle ride in the paddock, Daddy," Amanda announced. "It's such a lovely day, and the ground is softer now that the sun has melted the frost." Her father frowned. "Oh please, Daddy, I haven't been out on Saracen for ages, and the exercise will do them both good."

"Oh, let them go, Charles, just for an hour," said Amanda's mother. "The fresh air will do them good. But listen, Amanda, if you see any frozen patches in the paddock, you mustn't ride the ponies … just walk them. I don't want either of them to damage a leg. Do you understand?"

"Yes, Mammy, we'll be careful ... promise." She moved towards her father's armchair. He looked up from reading his paper.

"That Bartlett fellow, dear," he muttered, holding up the front page to show his wife. "They're still hunting for him, and now they've found another piece of his poor wife. The bastard should be horse-whipped when they find him."

"Charles," she frowned, "mind your language in front of the girls. He came to one of our parties, didn't he?" He glanced at Amanda.

"What now, Amanda?"

"The key, Daddy, may I have the key to the shed? I need my tack." He placed the newspaper on the arm of the chair, got up and went into the kitchen, returning with a bunch of keys.

"It's this one, Amanda. Make sure that you lock the shed again when you've finished." He handed her a can of de-icer. "Just in case the padlock is frozen," he explained.

"Thanks, Daddy." Smiling, she and Mary left the lounge. He watched them leave, then looked across the room.

"Yes, dear, the Bartletts did come to one of our parties. He was a total bore, a jumped-up jeweller from Scarborough way, but his wife was a damned good-looking filly, common, but very attractive."

"Charles!" She stood up and watched the two girls as they made their way to the paddock. They passed the stable, then continued to the corner of the paddock, heading for the large shed, where a dog-leg in the field took them out of sight.

"I'm really looking forward to this," Amanda spoke to Mary, making shapes with her frosty breath. "We haven't been riding for ages."

"The ground is fine, I think."

"Oh yes, the ponies won't have any problems, but to be safe, we'll just let them have a gentle trot." She shivered. "God, it's sunny, but very cold. Are you OK, Mary?"

"I'm fine," she replied, as they neared the shed. Amanda checked the key, then tried it in the padlock. "It's a bit stiff," she muttered, squirting some de-icer on it, then she turned the key and opened the padlock. "Got it!" she smiled, looking at Mary. She swung open the door and entered the shed, squinting in the semi-darkness. Moving forward, she stumbled into something, stepped back, then screamed. Mary looked up and was violently sick. They both turned and ran for their lives, screaming at the top of their voices.

CHAPTER TWENTY-SEVEN

"I hope you all had a lovely weekend," Bentley grunted sarcastically, "because Dennis and I bloody didn't!" Slater nodded in support.

"What a mess!" he exclaimed. "Those poor girls will have nightmares for ages."

"Where were you all, anyway?" Bentley bellowed. "What's up with your mobiles?" he glared at Debbie Chapman. She paused to allow him to calm down.

"I was with a friend at a wedding in Leeds, Sir." He looked at Sharpe.

"At Laura's mother's in Hull, you know, with the baby." Then Ryan.

"Returning from Beamish, Sir, with Fiona."

"Well, make the most of your little breaks, because there won't be any bloody time off this week!" Bentley sat down, and consoled himself with a yellow jelly-baby. He looked for another before continuing. "As Dennis said, what a bloody mess! Two young girls from a big house near Malton found Bartlett hanging in a shed near their paddock. The door was padlocked, but he had broken the window, climbed on a water-butt and got inside. He hung his coat over the broken window, then strung himself up. How long do we think he'd been there, Dennis?"

"About two weeks, Sir."

"Well, you can imagine the state of the corpse … Jesus, what a shock for those two young girls! The cold weather helped to preserve the body, otherwise the forensic team could have just poured it into a body-bag." Chapman pulled a face, and looked out of the window. "Anyway, Angela's examining the body as we speak, but I don't think she'll have much more to tell us than we already know. Bartlett's dead, and he won't be giving us any information about Phoebe's killer."

"Did he leave a suicide note, Sir?" Ryan asked.

"Sort of," Bentley replied, looking at his notepad. "Just a scrap of paper in his coat pocket … *I'm so ashamed of what I've done.* Well, so are we, Mr bloody Bartlett, but what exactly have you done?"

"It could be a confession, Sir," Sharpe muttered, "there again, it could mean anything."

"Yes," Bentley continued, "he could be a lone killer, or he could have worked with someone else. We're no further forward." He looked angry.

"The extra publicity might bring some more responses, Sir," Ryan said quietly.

"The calls have started to come in this morning," Slater confirmed. "The weekend stories were all about Phoebe's leg, but tomorrow's paper will headline Bartlett's suicide."

"Yes, and people will be asking what we're doing about it," Bentley shouted. "Fuck all! That's what most people will be thinking."

"Have you heard from HQ, Sir?" Chapman asked.

"Oh yes, they've finished sniffing all of that bloody cannabis, so now the Chief Constable wants to know why we haven't solved this murder. He's threatened to send in an extra CID team." Bentley looked despondent.

"But it's our case, Sir," Chapman stated angrily.

"Well, yes, it is … for now. We need to get a breakthrough … and quickly." He stood up. "We can't sit moping in here, so Debbie, I want you to come with me to interview the Griffiths at Malton. The rest of you, keep chasing those calls. We'll meet again here at 4 o'clock, OK?"

***

Bentley and Chapman were ushered into a large, spacious lounge, but were not offered any refreshments. "How is your daughter, Mrs Griffiths, and the other girl?" Bentley asked quietly.

"How do you think, Inspector?" No reply. "She's totally distraught, and so is Mary. They've had to be sedated, but they're going to have horrible nightmares for the months to come … years, even."

"Bloody man, hanging himself there like that," Charles Griffiths spoke angrily, "he disappeared weeks ago, so why haven't you tracked him down before now?"

"This has been a very difficult case, Mr Griffiths," Chapman took up the reins, "and we're doing all we can to find Mrs Bartlett's killer, or killers. We had hoped that Mr Bartlett would be able to provide us with some vital information, but now … We know that he was involved, but we have other suspects in mind."

"Other suspects!" Griffiths shouted, "Surely it's obvious that Bartlett murdered his wife, then couldn't cope with the guilt?" He paused. "I was going to say that they should bring back hanging, but the bastard has saved you the trouble!" They all relaxed.

"Had you met Bartlett before, Mr Griffiths?" Chapman asked.

"Yes, we have," she answered, "he and his wife attended one of our summer parties, didn't they, Charles?"

"That's right, the summer before last. I had purchased some expensive jewellery for my wife from one of his shops, and I already knew one of his golfing friends, Harold Hardy from Filey, so I invited them all to my wife's birthday party in August. We had a marquee on the paddock." He reflected for a few seconds. "I remember his wife, a good-looking woman …"

"Mutton dressed as lamb, darling. She had no breeding at all, Charles … common as muck, as they say."

"Quite right, dear," Griffiths answered sensibly, "they weren't the sort we normally mingle with, but, well, it was just a one-off. That's the only time we met them, I'm pretty sure of that." Bentley nodded.

"I think that's all for now. The forensics team ought to have finished by this evening, then, I hope, you can get back to normal."

"Normal?" Griffiths spluttered. "There won't be any normal for quite some time, Detective Inspector. For a start, I'll have to demolish that shed." He grimaced. "It's all very inconvenient."

"We'll see ourselves out," Chapman announced, and she and Bentley stood up, and left.

***

"Let's get started," Bentley muttered, glancing at his watch. "Debbie and I had a rather tetchy meeting with the Griffiths this morning. Mr Griffiths seemed to be more concerned with the inconvenience Bartlett's suicide had caused, rather than his daughter's feelings."

"What inconvenience?" Sharpe asked.

"He's got to demolish the shed where Bartlett hanged himself," Chapman replied. "Most inconvenient," she added sarcastically.

"Was Bartlett a friend of theirs?" said Ryan.

"No, George, the Bartletts had been invited to one of their summer parties."

"Yes," Bentley continued, "a posh do, with tents, and everything."

"A marquee, Sir," Chapman reminded him.

"Oh yes, so Bartlett must have noticed the shed where they stored a lot of the horsey stuff, but I can't understand why he trailed all of the way to Malton to top himself. There must be a lot of sheds much nearer to home than that."

"Perhaps he thought that it would take some time before his body was discovered," Ryan mused, "time which would be useful to an accomplice."

"Maybe," Sharpe continued, "but we still don't know whether there was an accomplice."

"True," Chapman conceded, "but it's still hard to believe that Bartlett killed his wife and dismembered her body all on his own. He must have had somebody helping him." The nods suggested that the others agreed with her.

"But who?" Bentley stoked his chin. "That's the big question." He looked at Slater. "Any useful calls, Dennis?"

"Nothing exciting, Sir, but Tim received a call about half an hour ago."

"That's right, from Jim Goodman, one of Galbraith's crew. He said he had some information for me."

"What kind of information?"

"He wouldn't say, Sir. He lives at Robin Hoods Bay, and I've arranged to see him in the morning."

"Good, well go straight there, Tim. Don't bother calling in here before you go. If there's anything that you urgently need to know, I'll ring your mobile. Make sure that you've got the bloody thing with you this time!" He looked around the room. "I'll have an initial forensics report tomorrow morning," Bentley informed the team. "Is there anything else?" Silence. "No, OK then, get yourselves home, have a rest, and come back raring to go tomorrow morning!"

CHAPTER TWENTY-EIGHT

Tim Sharpe found a space in the car park at the top of New Road at Robin Hoods Bay, and prepared himself for the steep descent down the hill. It was very windy, and was raining slightly, so he fastened his coat, pulled up the hood, and got on his way. There was no-one around to ask for directions, but about halfway down, he spotted a narrow lane on the left, and walked slowly along it, looking for *Wayfarer,* Jim Goodman's cottage. As he neared it, he noticed the burly fisherman standing just inside the front door, and Sharpe quickly followed him into the warmth of the lounge.

"God, it's a wild day," Sharpe grinned, taking off his coat.

"You get used to it, living around here," Goodman replied. "Coffee?"

"Please, milk and two sugars." Sharpe settled down, and rummaged for his pen and notepad. Goodman returned with a steaming mug, and sat down opposite Sharpe, who was rubbing his eyes.

"Tired?"

"Just a bit … we've got a three-weeks-old baby girl, and it was my turn last night."

"Those days are behind me, thank God."

"Now, you said that you had some information for me, Jim. Why all the secrecy?"

"We fishermen belong to a close-knit community, and I didn't want anyone to see me talking to you in Whitby." He smiled. "You never know when you might be looking for a new boat."

"OK, that's fine with me, so what do you have to tell me?"

"When you last saw me in Whitby, you asked if I had seen or heard anything unusual about Tom Galbraith. I like the skipper, and nothing sprang to mind at the time, but when I read the stories about his brother-in-law Arthur Bartlett and how you had found parts of Phoebe's body, that rang a bell. It was our first trip out this year, and Galbraith was taking the early morning shift. I was fast asleep, but I heard a noise and stood on the top of the steps to have a quick look round. I saw Galbraith manoeuvring a large package at the stern of the boat, and as I watched, he heaved it overboard then turned around. I ducked down, then got back to my bed." He smiled briefly. "I've seen crewmen bring all kinds of things on board to dump in the North Sea … old bikes, bags of rubbish, bits of scrap … so I didn't think twice about it at the time."

"How big was the package, Jim?"

"It was oblong, a good yard or so long, a couple of feet wide … something like that … quite bulky, I would say." He held out his arms to demonstrate.

"OK, could you see what it was?"

"No, it was wrapped in black plastic, or similar."

"Right, did Galbraith ever mention the package to you, or to one of the others?"

"No, I assumed that he didn't see me. It was only half-light, and I'd only poked my head above the deck level." He paused, and continued seriously. "That's all I've got to tell you, DC Sharpe, but this has got to be confidential, you understand? I don't want Tom to find out it was me that told you this story, and then to lose my job because he just chucked a dead dog over the side. He's a good skipper and I love my job, so don't fuck it up for me … alright?"

"Don't worry, Jim, we'll be very careful and only use your information if we think Galbraith has something to hide."

"I read in the paper this morning that you've found Bartlett's body."

"Yes, that's true, but not Phoebe's killer." Sharpe drained his coffee and stood up to leave. "Many thanks, Jim," he said, holding up his notepad, "this could be invaluable."

***

The team sat and listened carefully to Sharpe's summary of his meeting with Jim Goodman. "Wow, this really blows the case wide open, doesn't it?" Chapman exclaimed. "We speculated before that Galbraith may have had a fling with Phoebe, or had been rebuffed by her … hence his hatred for her. His wife hated her as well, she may even have found out about Phoebe flirting with her husband, so either he conspired with Bartlett to kill Phoebe, or the three of them did."

"It's also likely that Galbraith had the skill and the nerve to dismember her body," Sharpe suggested, "as he was used to cutting up fish in his job."

"Goodman's description of the package suggests that it may have been Phoebe's torso," Slater continued, "and he probably wrapped weights in it to keep it on the seabed."

"Where it might still be recovered by another trawler?" Sharpe added. "What do you think, Sir?"

"If we bring him in, Sharpie, he'll probably deny everything, because he knows that Bartlett can't implicate him, and without the package we have no evidence." He looked at Ryan. "You're quiet, George. What do you think about this, and why did you need to return to Filey this morning?"

"I don't think we can single out Galbraith, Sir. If he was the killer who dismembered Phoebe's body, why didn't he take all of her body parts and dump them at sea? Why would he allow Bartlett to keep his wife's head in the freezer, where it was likely to be found when she had been missing for some time? Why would he travel to the old mansion grounds near Scarborough just to bury one of her legs? It doesn't make sense to me. No, Galbraith wasn't the killer, but he may have been one of her killers." He paused and looked at Bentley. "May I explain, Sir? What I have to say may sound a bit far-fetched, but I think I have most of the evidence to support my ideas, even if some aspects may need to be double-checked."

"That's alright, George, we're all ears." Bentley smiled to himself, watching the young DC thinking outside the box.

"We know that Phoebe Bartlett was alive at the New Year party, but we can't be sure exactly when she died. We also know who remained at the party after the neighbours and the fishermen left – Arthur Bartlett, his sister Barbara and her husband Tom Galbraith, Phoebe's sister Melissa Jordan, Bartlett's best friend Harold Hardy, and the local farmer Frank Parkinson. We've also got good reasons to believe that all of those people probably hated Phoebe ... some because they thought she was a gold-digger, the men who may have had a fling with her or had been rebuffed and humiliated by her, and Melissa because she was jealous of her sister. Bartlett had long given Phoebe freedom in her private life, and almost certainly knew that she had been unfaithful. He either did not want to know about her affairs, or had forgiven her for them, but it's pretty clear that he did love Phoebe, so why was she killed? I think it's likely that the well-publicised affair with the footballer Jack Mason tipped the balance, and that one, two or all of the others put pressure on Bartlett to agree to or participate in her murder."

"All of them, George?" Chapman exclaimed, looking mystified. "There's not a shred of evidence for that."

"Until last night I would have agreed with you, Debbie, but this …" he flourished Amelia Archer's sketchbook "… is a silent witness." Bentley smiled as the others looked puzzled.

"What the hell is that?" Sharpe shrugged his shoulders melodramatically.

"This sketchbook, Tim, belongs to Amelia Archer, the deaf mute who is our silent witness. Amelia may not be able to hear or to speak, but she can communicate by sign language, and by her sketches. She is a very talented artist for her age. I asked Mrs Archer if I could borrow this book over a week ago, but we've been so busy that I didn't have a proper look at it until last night. The book mainly contains Amelia's drawings of animals, her family, familiar buildings and so on, but it was Fiona Charlton who first noticed an unusual sketch the other day, and pointed it out to me. Here are some copies of that sketch, which I showed to DI Bentley." He passed them around, and the others peered at the drawing of the white van.

"Yes, George gave me a copy of this sketch, and when we discussed it, we realised that it showed a white van travelling to Parkinson's farm. You can see the sign for the farm behind the van. We knew that Parkinson didn't own a van like this, so we thought it must be connected to the cannabis farm. I sent a copy to HQ, and they used the lettering to track down one of Parkinson's accomplices in Hull."

"Impressive, George," Slater muttered, "so what other clues are in the book?"

"There's a nice sketch of the New Year fireworks display, and a portrait of Phoebe that Amelia must have drawn a day or two before." He passed more copies around the room.

"It's a good likeness of Phoebe," Chapman conceded.

"This is the key sketch, I think," Ryan continued. "It was drawn some time before New Year." He gave each of the team a copy of a simpler drawing, which showed a group of people, some sitting, some standing.

"What's special about this, George?" Sharpe asked. "It's just six people socialising."

"Hmm," Bentley added, "it looks like four men and two women."

"Exactly, Sir," Ryan continued, "and no prizes for guessing which six people."

"The people who disliked Phoebe," answered Sharpe, "but as I said before, what's so special about this sketch? They could be just having a meal or a drink, or playing cards … nothing criminal there."

"True, Tim, but as I said before, this sketch was drawn before New Year. Where is Phoebe? There isn't a woman with blonde hair, so why wasn't she involved? Could it be that they were plotting Phoebe's murder?"

"You are way off the mark, George, we don't know exactly who these people were, or where they were meeting." Sharpe looked for a response.

"Yes, we do, Tim, because, if you look carefully, this sketch is looking down at the group of people, and I believe that Amelia was kneeling by her landing window when she drew it. I checked it out today. The six people are in Bartlett's conservatory."

"We still can't prove it was them, George."

"No, not yet, but when Amelia returns from boarding school next weekend, we can ask her mother to see if Amelia can identify any of them."

"Yes," muttered Debbie Chapman, peering at the sketch again. "I think that man with rough hair could be the farmer, Frank Parkinson, and the woman …"

"OK, Debbie," Bentley interrupted her, "let's not play guessing games. What else have you got, George?"

"There's one more sketch, Sir. It was just in one corner of a page, but it had been drawn after the New Year party." He handed another copy to each of the team.

"What the hell is that?" Slater asked. "It looks like an axe or something similar." The drawing appeared to show something in a small window in a dark building.

"Yes, that one intrigued me as well, Dennis, but something looked familiar to me. Debbie, when we visited Parkinson's farm, do you remember passing a large shed?"

"Hmm, I think so … before the farmyard?"

"Yes, well I went for a look this morning, and I think a little girl, looking up at the window in the shed from across the lane, would have had this view."

"We thought Parkinson may have used that shed,

years ago when he kept animals, as an abattoir," Chapman said thoughtfully.

"So what's going on in the drawing," Sharpe asked, "is Parkinson chopping up something?"

"You may have hit the nail on the head, Tim," Ryan nodded slowly. There was a minute or two of quiet contemplation as the team tried to take in all of the information that Ryan had provided. Bentley suddenly remembered his jelly-babies, selected a black one, ate it, then broke the silence.

"Let's see if I've got this right, George. You think that the six people shown in Amelia's sketch of the conservatory plotted to murder Phoebe? We know from the forensic evidence that Phoebe was poisoned, and we know from the body parts discovered so far that Bartlett, probably Galbraith and possibly someone else were involved in getting rid of them. If Galbraith did throw Phoebe's torso into the North Sea, then we still have three body parts to find … her left leg and both of her arms. The other sketch that you found suggests that Phoebe's body was dismembered in Parkinson's shed." He paused for a moment of reflection. "OK so far?"

"Yes, that's fine, Sir." Ryan replied, then he turned to look at Sharpe, who continued the summary.

"I get all of that, Sir, I can see that we can build up a case against some, or all, of that group of six for being an accessory to murder, but what I would like to know, and what we need to find out, is who actually poisoned her."

"Good thinking, Tim," Bentley smiled, "well done. We could arrest the remaining five tomorrow morning, grill them and hope that one of them will break down and reveal the name of the poisoner, but I think it better to try to build up our evidence before we do that."

"We need to check Lamb Rigg Farm, Sir … the abattoir?" Slater suggested.

"Well, yes, Dennis, but not just the shed … the farmhouse and other outer buildings as well. HQ's searches concentrated on the cannabis farm, but I want to find out what else Parkinson was up to. I'll arrange for a search team and the forensics people to go in first thing in the morning, and Tim … you can come along with me. Dennis, sorry, but can you hold the fort again here? Debbie and George, phone Mrs Archer now and see if she is available to go with you to Amelia's school. Take her sketchbook, and try to identify as many people as you can in it. Did she date any of the drawings, George?"

"No, she didn't, Sir, but I think we can assume that all of the drawings before the fireworks sketch are from last year, when Phoebe was still alive."

"OK. Anything else?"

"Don't you think, Sir," Chapman asked, "that whatever evidence we find, the others will cover their backs and just blame Bartlett for the murder?"

"I'm sure they will try to do that, but if we can find out who supplied the poison, who posed as Phoebe on the security camera, and who chopped her up … then we'll be able to put so much pressure on them that someone will crack." He checked the papers on his desk. "Right, I think that's everything for now, so let's make sure that we get some results tomorrow." He stood up to go.

"One last thing, Sir."

"Yes, George, what is it?"

"I do have another theory to put to you, but I need to check something in Bartlett's house before I do. Will that be OK?"

"There's no-one there to stop you, George. Pick up the keys before you call for Mrs Archer."

***

George drove past Debbie Chapman's house on his way back to his flat. No red car in the street. He decided to do a daily check. Perhaps Henderson was just confirming that Fiona had a boyfriend and another life? He drove along the street and turned his thoughts to the following morning.

CHAPTER TWENTY-NINE

A pale winter sun gazed down on the yard and buildings of Lamb Rigg Farm as Bentley's squad of searchers and forensics experts parked their vehicles. It was a chilly morning, and Sharpe shivered as he waited for Bentley to get out of the car and issue instructions to the others. The yard was quiet, as Parkinson's dog had been taken away, and his mother was now in a care home. Bentley spoke to the forensics team first, and they entered the former abattoir, so Sharpe unlocked the farmhouse and beckoned for the two searchers to join him in the lounge. After a few minutes, he could hear Bentley's footsteps in the kitchen. "We're through here, Sir," Sharpe called.

"OK, lads, we need to go through this place with a fine toothcomb. Forget about the barns, the team from York will have picked them clean, but I want you to ransack this place, then check the other small buildings and sheds outside. You're looking for anything that could link Parkinson to Phoebe

Bartlett – letters, photos, clothing, even a missing leg or arm. The York team have already made a mess here, searching for evidence that would lead them to Parkinson's accomplices, so don't worry about causing more mess … after all, nobody lives here now. The forensic team are concentrating on the abattoir, looking for any trace of Phoebe's blood." He looked around. "It's bloody freezing here, so let's get on with it."

***

Debbie Chapman drew the car to a halt outside the Archers' home, and Ryan glanced over to *Mandalay*. "I won't be too long, Debbie, so please keep Mrs Archer occupied until I get back."

"Don't spend ages chasing your little theories, Georgie-Boy, we've got a long day ahead of us as it is." She smiled and headed for the Archers' house, as Ryan walked to *Mandalay* and unlocked the padlocks securing the outer gate and the front door. He shivered as he entered the house, then made for the kitchen. Ryan spent almost twenty minutes in checking the range of cupboards in the kitchen, then did the same in the dining room and the conservatory. He double-checked the kitchen again, nodded thoughtfully and smiled to himself, then he carefully locked the premises and made the short walk to re-join Chapman and Mrs Archer.

***

"Any luck, Sir?" Sharpe asked, rubbing his hands together. "I could do with a nice hot mug of coffee and a chocolate éclair," he added, smiling at the DI.

"Oh, I'll just go and rustle one up in the kitchen," Bentley replied sarcastically. "We're done downstairs, so I'll go outside into the cold air, Tim," he smiled, "and see how the forensics people are getting on. You can nip upstairs and give the bedrooms a last check, but make sure you pull everything to bits this time. I've got a feeling that Parkinson still has some secrets hidden in this place." He fastened his coat, and disappeared out of the farmhouse door, as Sharpe shuffled his way upstairs. He pulled out every drawer in the four bedrooms, throwing them onto the beds, and thoroughly examined underneath and behind each one. Sharpe did the same with the bedside table, looking carefully behind each one, then he crawled under each bed, coughing as he disturbed the heavy dust.

Dirty bastard! he thought, as he dusted himself down and began putting things back in their place. As he was manoeuvring a medium-sized cabinet back into its corner, he tilted it and noticed an A4 brown envelope, taped to the back. Sharpe sat on the bed and opened the envelope, spilling out the contents onto the duvet. He picked up a magazine, browsed through it, then flicked at a smaller packet filled with colour photos. *What a body!* He grinned to himself, then had another look at the magazine, popped everything back into the envelope, and carried it downstairs. Sharpe opened the farmhouse door, spotted Bentley and two of the forensics team near a wall on the far side of the farmyard, and shouted: "Sir, come and see what I've found here!" He brandished the brown envelope.

***

Amelia Archer and her mother, and Chapman and Ryan sat around a bright green table in a common room at Amelia's school. Her teacher had shown the police officers around the school, while Mrs Archer had a quiet word with her daughter before joining the two police officers. Some glasses of water and orange squash were on the table, and Amelia's sketchbook lay in the middle. Mrs Archer used spoken questions and sign language to act as a go-between her daughter and the police. Ryan began by indicating two of the portraits of Phoebe, and watched the conversation.

"Phoebe lives next door to us, and Amelia loves her very much. She often goes inside Phoebe's house, especially in the summer." *Amelia still doesn't know that Phoebe is dead*, Ryan thought to himself, then he smiled and turned a few pages to the sketch of the white van. He watched mother and daughter again.

"This van is going to Mr Parkinson's farm," she said. "Amelia has seen this van and a larger white van going into the farm, but when she tried to go near the farm, one of the men from the van told her to go away." Ryan nodded, and moved a few pages forward to the drawing of the six people.

"This was at Phoebe's house. Amelia could see them from an upstairs window in our house."

"Have you seen any of the people before, Amelia?" Ryan asked. Mother and daughter conferred again.

"Amelia knows Mr Bartlett, Phoebe's husband. He is quite an old man." Ryan and Chapman smiled at the young girl. "Mr Parkinson was there as well … the man from the farm, and Amelia has seen one of the women before," she pointed at one of the figures in the sketch, "but she does not know who she is. She does not know who the other people are, but thinks that they may have been at the New Year party at the Bartletts' house." Ryan nodded and turned a few pages to the fireworks drawing.

"This is at Phoebe's house. Amelia likes the fireworks very much." Her daughter smiled excitedly. "She stayed up very late that night. Amelia hasn't seen Phoebe since the party." She frowned.

"Does she know that Phoebe has gone away?"

"Yes, DC Ryan, that's what we have told her." Ryan moved on to the drawing with the axe. This time Amelia looked frightened. She signed her mother.

"It was dark, and at Mr Parkinson's farm. She could see a light in the shed, and saw somebody chopping something. The door opened and Amelia saw a shadow, so she crouched down at the side of the lane. The door closed again, and she ran home." Mrs Archer turned to Ryan. "I remember that night, DC Ryan, Amelia came tearing in to the house, crying. I tried to get her to tell me what was wrong, but she wouldn't say."

"OK," said Ryan. "Did Amelia recognise the

figure?" More signs.

"No, she couldn't see who it was." Ryan looked across the table at Chapman, who nodded, then he smiled at Amelia.

"You have been very helpful, Amelia, and your drawings are wonderful. Thank you very much," he said, smiling and taking a large bag of mixed sweets out of his pocket. "These are for you."

Amelia signed *Thank you*, and dragged the bag towards her. She stood up, gave Ryan and Chapman a hug, then left the room with her mother. "Well, that's confirmed some things, George, but has left a few question marks."

"Maybe, Debbie, but I still have my theories," he replied, grinning. They stood up and put on their coats, waiting for Mrs Archer to return.

***

Bentley and Sharpe sat in the kitchen, the magazine and photos spread on the table. "I guess that confirms some kind of relationship, Tim, but not necessarily an affair."

"OK, so she posed for him, but why *Limp Prick Farm*? Perhaps Phoebe got her kit off for Parkinson, then he couldn't perform, so she mocked him with the joke sign?"

"Yes, that sounds plausible, Tim."

"But look at her body, Sir … it would make a bishop kick a hole in a stained-glass window!" Sharpe joked, and even Bentley had to laugh. "If she'd been in front of me, bollock naked like that,

I would have been standing to attention and would definitely have performed!" Bentley grinned again as Sharpe added: "And I'm being polite, Sir!"

"Right, Sharpie, enough of the frivolities," Bentley became serious. "Put those photos back in the envelope, and don't try to nick any of them, then follow me outside. Forensics have found something." He returned to the farmyard, where the forensics team had gathered a few items in polythene bags. Bentley spoke to the older man in the team. "What have you found altogether, Bill?"

"We've taken some things from the shed … several samples of what might be blood, a cleaver, some knives, but we've also found some interesting things in that old oil drum over there." He pointed to a corner of the yard, well away from the house. "A number of items have been burned in there, Sir, so we've taken some samples. I'm pretty sure that some of them are bones, so we'll get Angela Collins to check them out." He looked at Bentley and Sharpe. "Fingers crossed, eh?"

"Good work, Bill. Now let's get back to base and find a hot drink!"

CHAPTER THIRTY

"We made some interesting discoveries at Parkinson's farm yesterday," Bentley opened the briefing, standing in front of the glamour shots of Phoebe Bartlett which Sharpe had pinned on the incident board.

"It's alright, Sir," Chapman grinned, looking at Sharpe, "I've seen the girlie pictures. Better men than him," she gestured in Sharpe's direction, "have tried to embarrass me and failed!" The others laughed politely.

"I found the photos in an envelope taped behind one of Parkinson's bedside cabinets," Sharpe explained. "I think that Parkinson persuaded Phoebe to do some glamour modelling for him, then tried to get it up … and failed." He smiled at the others.

"Whereas you, Sharpie …" Chapman laughed scornfully, then continued. "Have these photos got something to do with that *Limp Prick* sign, Sir?"

"Probably, Debbie, if Sharpe's right," Bentley

replied. "That would explain why Parkinson hated her so much … but more importantly, forensics found possible traces of blood in that shed, and some burnt items, including bones, in an old oil drum in the farmyard. They're running checks this morning, and will let us know as soon as possible. It looks as if your theory about Parkinson dismembering Phoebe in the shed could be right, George."

"That's good, Sir. Amelia told us, through sign language of course, that the hellish sketch with the axe was at Parkinson's shed, but she ran away when someone came outside. She couldn't identify who it was."

"But she did identify some of the six people in the conservatory drawing," Chapman continued, "including Arthur Bartlett, Frank Parkinson, and said that two were women. She thought that most, if not all of them, were at the New Year party."

"Amelia also told us that more than one white van had visited the farm, but couldn't provide any more details about them."

"Hmm, so putting George's theories to one side for a moment," Bentley glanced around at the others, "I think we have a very strong case against Parkinson as being the killer. Firstly, he hated Phoebe for teasing him, then humiliating him." He put up one finger. "Secondly, he had the support of the other conspirators who provided the location for the murder, and helped him distribute the body parts. They all had reasons for wanting her dead as well." Two fingers. "Thirdly, it looks likely that

Parkinson dismembered the body in his shed. He had the knowledge to do this, and would not have been too squeamish about doing it." Three. "He had access to strychnine from one of his farmer mates, who would have used it as rat poison." Four. "Is there anything else?"

"Phoebe may have known about his cannabis farm, and could have been blackmailing him," Sharpe added. "It's just another reason for wanting her out of the way."

"What about the poison, Sir?" Slater asked. "Was any found by the forensic team?"

"We'll have to wait and see, Dennis, but in any case, it's quite likely that Parkinson dumped it somewhere after the murder."

"Have we got enough evidence for the CPS to proceed against Parkinson as the killer, and the others as accessories?" Chapman asked. "As Dennis said, we haven't got the poison, and there's only circumstantial evidence against the others as fellow-conspirators."

"What about Phoebe's head in Bartlett's freezer?" Sharpe said.

"Christ, yes, I'd forgotten about that," Chapman confessed. "OK, then, perhaps Bartlett is the only accessory to murder. He was under a lot of pressure from the others to do something about Phoebe's promiscuity, and he knew he could rely on Parkinson to do the dirty deed for him. After the event, he was so ashamed of what he'd done that he topped himself."

"And the torso in the sea?" Slater questioned.

"Circumstantial, Dennis," Bentley replied, "unless, of course, it turns up in a trawler's net. Then we've got proof that some of the others were involved. At the moment, if we challenge Galbraith, he'll just say that it was some rubbish that went overboard." He thought for a moment. "Parkinson's going down for the cannabis farm, and we've got enough proof that he helped with the disposal of the body, but if he denies being the killer, we haven't got any evidence to nail him on that."

"Even with the poison, Sir, he could still deny being the killer. He could argue that he supplied Bartlett with the poison, and agreed to dispose of the body, but still insist that Bartlett was the killer." Sharpe sat back in his chair. "It's easy to blame a dead man. The others could all argue that it was Bartlett's brainchild, and that they knew nothing about his arrangement with Parkinson."

"Right, we could just sit around on our arses until we get some reports from forensics," Bentley muttered sternly, "but I think that Parkinson may spill the beans if we lean on him with the evidence that we already have, and then offer him a possible reduced term if he co-operates with us. Debbie, you can come with me to the remand centre at York. The rest of you have got reports to do, so get on with them! Dennis … phone me as soon as you get any info from forensics, OK?"

"What about George's theories, Sir" Chapman asked. "Should we listen …?"

"They can wait until later, Debbie," Ryan interrupted her. "You may get lucky with Parkinson, in which case you won't need my ideas. All that I'll say for now, Sir, is that I think Parkinson will deny being the killer, and so will the others if you interview them."

"So you think Bartlett poisoned his wife?" Bentley muttered, looking for his coat.

"No, Sir, I think he would have denied it as well." Bentley looked puzzled for a moment, then put on his coat.

"Come on, Debbie, let's go."

***

Bentley glared at Parkinson across the table, then looked at the warder standing outside the room. "Before we start, you are entitled to a solicitor if you wish. I will be asking you some awkward questions." Parkinson just shrugged.

"There's no need, Inspector … fire away."

"Yesterday, our forensics team conducted a thorough search of Lamb Rigg Farm. We weren't looking for more cannabis plants, or any other drugs, but for evidence which will help us convict Phoebe Bartlett's killer."

"Did you have a nice time?" Parkinson asked sarcastically.

"We found your collection of nude photos of Phoebe Bartlett hidden behind a bedside cabinet," Bentley announced.

"So what?" Parkinson said nonchalantly. "Phoebe was a glamour model. I taped them there because I didn't want my mother to find them. There's no law against owning a few glamour photos, is there? They weren't even pornographic."

"True, Frank, but you had a thing about Phoebe, didn't you? Did it hurt when she rejected you … humiliated you in front of your neighbours?"

"No!" Parkinson snapped.

"Made a fool of you, didn't she, Frank … made you angry, didn't it?

"No!"

"Teased you and made you so angry that you killed her, didn't you?" Parkinson made to stand up, red-faced. "Made you look small, didn't she, and you would have done anything to shut her up, wouldn't you?" Bentley shouted.

"No, I didn't kill her!"

"OK, so Phoebe found out about the cannabis farm and threatened to contact the police, so you killed her?"

"No, no, you're way off the mark."

"Well, if you didn't kill her, who did!" Parkinson clenched his fists, but didn't speak. A minute or so passed by. "Sit down, Frank, relax," Bentley ordered calmly. "Look, Frank, our forensics people were busy at your farm yesterday. They found traces of blood in your shed and on some knives, and some bone fragments. We know that you dismembered Phoebe's body in your shed, and that others helped you get rid of the body parts. We also know that she was poisoned, and that you obtained the strychnine from one of your farmer mates, so what are we to think? You plotted with others to kill Phoebe Bartlett, provided the poison which was used to kill her, then cut up her body. You're the bloody killer!" Parkinson suddenly looked deflated.

"Look, I won't deny that I was involved in her murder, but I'm telling you now, I didn't kill Phoebe!"

"Listen, Frank, we've got so much evidence against you that when they convict you for the drugs offences and now this, they'll just throw away the key." Bentley looked very calm. "They'll give you a really rough time in prison, Frank, they don't like men who kill women!" Parkinson sat back in his seat. "If you didn't murder Phoebe, why protect someone else who did?"

"I've told you the truth, Inspector, I didn't kill Phoebe." Parkinson looked at Bentley, then at Chapman. "I want to go back to my cell."

***

"Forensics have confirmed that spots of Phoebe's blood were on the floor of Parkinson's shed, and on his cleaver. They're still running tests on the burnt material found in the bottom of the oil drum, but they seem certain that some of it is coagulated black plastic."

"Similar to the type used to wrap the leg, Sir?" Sharpe asked.

"We'll know in a day or two but let's hope so. That would confirm Parkinson's role in disposing of one of Phoebe's body parts, and we're pretty certain that he dismembered the body."

"How did he react, Sir," Ryan said, "when you confronted him with all of this evidence?"

"He freely admitted that he was involved in the murder, but strongly denied that he killed Phoebe … as you said he would, George." They all looked at the young DC. "How did you know that he would deny it, George? I think it's time that you explained your big theory." Ryan glanced around, then moved to the incident board, where he could point to a particular reference or photo.

"Arthur Bartlett knew about his wife's affairs, and was prepared to tolerate them, even though his close family and best friend urged him to get rid of her. That changed when she had the fling with Jack Mason, which became public, and perhaps Bartlett finally realised that his wife didn't care if others knew that she was cheating on him, or worse, that she would leave him for good. It was becoming difficult for Bartlett to cover things up, and perhaps a comment was made here and there by members of his family or his friends, maybe in jest at first, but then the talk turned to a plan to get rid of Phoebe permanently. At some point Parkinson became involved, partly because he would be able to provide some practical help, also because Bartlett must have known that Phoebe had humiliated him in the past. This close circle met in December to finalise their plans, as Amelia's sketch shows." He pointed at the board, and paused for a moment to gather his thoughts. The others waited quietly. "The six plotters, who all hated Phoebe for various reasons, must have agreed at some point that they would all play an active part in the murder and disposal of the body, but they had to decide what method to use, and most importantly, who would do the killing."

"A difficult decision, George," Chapman interrupted. "It's all very well discussing a murder, but for one person to actually carry it out … that's must have been difficult."

"Exactly, Debbie. Parkinson told the others that he could obtain some strychnine, on the pretence of getting rid of a rat problem on his farm, and they all knew that the New Year party gave them an opportunity to administer the poison, but who would do it?"

"It could have been any of them," Sharpe muttered, "so who had the most guts?"

"None of them, Sharpie," Ryan answered, looking at Sharpe's blank face. "I thought that Parkinson would deny being the killer, and if you question the others, I think each one will deny it as well." The others looked puzzled. "Have you read that in the First World War and other conflicts, when they used firing squads for executions, there was a concern that the soldiers might be accused of murder at a later time, so it was decided that only one soldier would have a live cartridge in his rifle?" He paused briefly. "No-one could say which soldier had fired the live round, and I think something similar was agreed with Phoebe's murder. Before the party, each of the plotters was given a tiny packet of white, crystalline powder. One of the packets contained strychnine, the others a harmless substance. Mrs Galbraith mentioned to us that after the fireworks, when the neighbours had gone, some champagne flutes were filled with prosecco, Phoebe's favourite drink, and placed on a tray. The plotters had emptied their packets into separate glasses, so that no-one would know who had actually poisoned Phoebe. This is why each person could deny murder." The others looked at each other. "Nobody knows who poisoned Phoebe."

"We need to get forensics to check the champagne flutes," Chapman said, "to confirm that this was how the murder was committed."

"Too late, I'm afraid, Debbie" Ryan replied. "When I went to Bartlett's house yesterday, there wasn't a single champagne flute in the place. Somebody must have removed all of the glasses after the murder, and dumped them."

"And afterwards, George," Bentley smiled, "finish your story."

"On the third of January, Melissa or Barbara disguised herself and drove Phoebe's Mini away from the house. One of the plotters must have a contact in the car trade, and the plates could have been changed and the car sold on, or simply crushed. Around that time, Phoebe's body must have been taken to Parkinson's shed, where he dismembered it, as Amelia saw here." He pointed to the sketch. "Then, each of the six was given the responsibility of disposing of one part of Phoebe's body. I think that Hardy buried her right leg at *Abbotsfield*, in the old mansion grounds, Galbraith dumped the torso at sea, and Parkinson burnt an arm or a leg. We might know which tomorrow. Melissa and Barbara probably dumped their parts somewhere, perhaps on the moors, and Arthur Bartlett, of course, was given his wife's head. The trouble was that Bartlett must have regretted agreeing to Phoebe's murder, and he couldn't bring himself to get rid of her head. He might not even have looked at it after the head was placed in his freezer. The guilt of what he had done slowly gnawed into him, until he decided to take his own life. He perhaps did not intend betraying his fellow-murderers, but by leaving the head in the freezer, he provided us with an opening in the case. From that point, with help from little Amelia, we've been able to break down the case and find out what must have happened." Ryan glanced at the incident board, then returned to his desk.

"Well done, George!" Chapman patted his arm enthusiastically.

"Brilliant, young Ryan," Sharpe conceded, "you've done well, but do we have the evidence to convince the CPS to prosecute the five who are left?"

"Good point, Sharpie," Bentley bellowed, "but after tomorrow we will." He looked at the others. "First thing in the morning, I'll go to Whitby with Tim, arrest Tom and Barbara Galbraith, and bring them back to Northway in separate cars. Debbie, take George to Filey and arrest Hardy. Dennis, you can stay here, and act as liaison, OK? I'll contact the team at Thirsk to arrest Melissa Jordan, and bring her here to Scarborough nick. We'll keep them stewing in separate cells until the afternoon."

"On what charge, Sir?" Chapman asked.

"Murder for now, Debbie. If what George told us is right, I don't know what charge would stick … maybe accessory to murder. We'll have to get the bloody CPS to look it up!"

"And if we don't get one of them to confess, Sir, what then …?" Slater asked.

"One of them will crack, Dennis, don't you worry about that. We'll use stick and carrot, bully and bluff, until someone breaks down, and we've still got Parkinson as a fallback." He pondered for a moment. "I don't think it will come to that, Dennis … after an hour or two in those shitholes downstairs, they'll say anything to get out!"

***

The following morning, at seven o'clock, Tom and Barbara Galbraith, and Melissa Jordan were roused from their beds, arrested, and brought to Scarborough police station. Harold Hardy was already up and dressed, ready to play an early round of golf, when he was arrested by Chapman and Ryan, and brought to Northway for questioning.

Bentley decided that he and Ryan would interview the women, leaving Chapman and

Sharpe to question Galbraith and Hardy. It was early afternoon before the interviews began, and by then Barbara Galbraith in particular was in a very distressed state. The team had expected the men to be defiant, which they were, but Bentley told Debbie Chapman not to use the information from the crewman in the interview. Sharpe still needed to obtain a formal statement from the fisherman, and that could be used at a second interview if necessary. Melissa Jordan also proved to be stubborn, taking her solicitor's advice to answer no comment to most of the questions. That left Barbara Galbraith, and it was almost three o'clock when she faced Bentley and Ryan across the table.

"Mrs Galbraith, this morning we arrested you and your husband, Harold Hardy, and Melissa Jordan for the murder of your sister-in-law, Phoebe Bartlett. I would like you to tell me about your part in the murder." Bentley spoke firmly and calmly.

"I don't have anything to tell you, Inspector," she answered nervously. "I had nothing to do with the murder of Phoebe." She glanced at her solicitor, who nodded.

"Since we last spoke to you about the disappearance of Mrs Bartlett, we have gathered considerable evidence … positive evidence that she did not go away on holiday, but was brutally murdered in her own house by someone after the New Year party which took place there. We know that she was alive at the end of the party, but that she died soon afterwards." Bentley continued his slow summary.

"We have since recovered one of her legs, and her head, Mrs Galbraith … the head of your sister-in-law which was hacked off and hidden by your brother in his freezer." Bentley sat back as Barbara Galbraith paled. "We know that you didn't like Phoebe, but somebody brutally carved her body into six pieces, which were then scattered around North Yorkshire, Mrs Galbraith … and I believe that you not only took part in her murder, but also got rid of one of the body parts!" Reddening, Barbara Galbraith glanced quickly at her solicitor, then muttered something quietly, tears forming in her eyes.

"What did you say?"

"I said that I didn't kill her."

"You didn't kill her, Mrs Galbraith, but you dumped part of her body?"

"Really, Detective Inspector," the solicitor interrupted, wiping his glasses, "what a fantastic accusation. Where is your evidence for this?" Bentley ignored him.

"Where did you dump the package, Mrs Galbraith?" No answer, just tears.

"Look, Barbara," Bentley continued quietly, "we know all about the poison. Frank Parkinson has been very talkative … singing like a canary, in fact." He smiled briefly. "He has told us all about the strychnine, and how it was placed in a glass of prosecco." He paused to let the information sink in. "Parkinson has also admitted that he dismembered

Phoebe's body … your brother's wife … and prepared six packages, two of which we have already found, and another which we suspect is in the North Sea." He glared at her, then nudged Ryan, who pushed Amelia's sketch of the chopping scene across the table. "You see, Barbara, that we have a witness." She blanched visibly, and put her hand over her mouth. "A fishing vessel will probably find that package in the North Sea, Mrs Galbraith, and I think you know who dumped it there." Bentley looked at her again, then spoke to Ryan. "DC Ryan, ask the constable to bring Mrs Galbraith a glass of water." Ryan stood up, moved to the door, and spoke to the officer outside the interview room. Bentley waited until he gave the glass to Mrs Galbraith, who drank half of it quickly. "I ask you again, Mrs Galbraith, to describe the part you played in Phoebe Bartlett's murder." She shook her head, and began crying.

"I can't," she muttered between sobs, "I didn't kill her."

"Barbara," Bentley spoke softly again, "we know exactly what happened, but if you don't tell us your part, then it will go really badly for you when you are sentenced." He paused. "And it will be the same for your husband. If you co-operate with us, and tell us the truth, the judge will take this into consideration and your prison term could be much shorter." Barbara Galbraith calmed down slowly, then sat up in her seat.

"No comment." Ryan could feel the anger rising in Bentley next to him. The DI sorted through the papers in a wallet file, and placed Amelia's sketch of the group meeting on the table.

"You're wasting our time, Mrs Galbraith." He jabbed at the sketch. "We have a witness who saw the six of you plotting in Bartlett's conservatory to murder his wife!" he stated angrily.

"Detective Inspector, I must protest," the solicitor spoke again. "A childish drawing, what kind of evidence is this?" Bentley ignored him again.

"You and your husband met with Harold Hardy, Melissa Jordan, Frank Parkinson and your brother in his conservatory in December, and the six of you plotted the murder of Phoebe Bartlett." Bentley looked furious, as he reached in the wallet again. "You arranged to kill her at the New Year party, then Parkinson carved up her body and gave each of you a piece to get rid of somewhere in the county." Bentley pushed a photo of the leg found buried in the mound at *Abbotsfield* in front of her. The photo showed clearly that part of the foot has been gnawed by an animal. Galbraith reeled, and looked as if she was going to be sick. Bentley pressed again, finding another photo and shoving it in front of Galbraith. "Recognise her?" he bellowed, pointing at the head of Phoebe Bartlett with its black wrapping peeled away. Barbara Galbraith fainted, and Ryan dashed around the table to assist the solicitor in keeping her on the chair. Bentley stood up and found a box of tissues, moistening a few of them and passing them to the solicitor to press on Galbraith's forehead. After a few minutes, she came round, slowly composed herself, then sat up and turned the photos over.

"You go too far, Detective Inspector," the solicitor protested, "and if you do not have any real evidence, I must ask you to close this interview."

"We haven't finished yet," Bentley replied defiantly, then spoke quietly to Galbraith. "Look, Barbara, it isn't very pleasant when you are confronted with the reality of what you have done, is it? As I said before, we know what happened at *Mandalay* at New Year, and afterwards. All you have to do is to tell us everything … then your nightmare will be over." A sympathetic brief smile. "You will definitely feel a lot better if you are honest with us. I don't want to keep showing you these horrible photographs or to send you back to the cells for a few more hours, but I do want you to tell me exactly what happened." He looked at her as a kindly uncle would have done. "OK?"

"I didn't kill her, Inspector."

"I know, Barbara," he smiled, with an understanding look on his face, "because none of you knew which packet contained the poison. You all plotted to kill her without one person being singled out who got their hands dirty by being the actual killer. You passed the parcel around, then all of a sudden, Phoebe Bartlett was dead." She looked shocked. "As I have told you, Barbara, I know everything that happened." He glanced at Ryan, then Barbara Galbraith told them all that they needed to know.

CHAPTER THIRTY-ONE

"I want to begin this morning's briefing by saying *Well Done!*" Bentley smiled at everyone in the room and clapped his hands briefly. He then rewarded himself with a green jelly-baby. "We still have a lot of work ahead of us, but I'm really proud of the effort that you all have put in over the past weeks since Jack Mason first reported Phoebe Bartlett as a missing person. At times, I think we all wondered whether we were on a wild goose chase, but we've persevered and worked hard, and finally got the result." The others now clapped and smiled at each other. "Don't get too carried away," Bentley warned, "because we still have a few loose ends to tie up, and a lot of reports to write." Groans.

"Have you had a chance to speak to the CPS yet, Boss?" Sharpe asked. "I was just wondering what charges they will apply."

"Good question, Sharpie. I will make a call today, but I don't think that this notion they had of being innocent of murder will wash with the CPS. This firing squad idea that George mentioned is bullshit as far as I'm concerned."

"The way I see it, Sir," Ryan responded to the mention of his name, "is that everything they did … the plotting, the poison, the glasses of prosecco, and the disposal of the body parts … was all done with intent to kill. They are all guilty of murder in my book."

"I'm sure that we all agree, George, but it's down to the CPS now. We just have to help them by obtaining more confessions, and by looking to build up the evidence against them. Barbara Galbraith has provided us with a few leads. She reckoned that Melissa Jordan disguised herself as Phoebe, then drove away in the Mini to Hardy's house in Filey. He had contacts in Newcastle, she thought, who would get rid of the car. We need to pressurise Hardy, to check some of his golfing friends, and to find out if he has any contacts or business interests in Newcastle. You can make a start on that one, Dennis." He paused to check his notepad. "Sharpie, that fisherman, Jim Goodman, we need a statement from him, OK?" Sharpe nodded. "We're still short of a leg and an arm, now that forensics have confirmed that the bone fragments at the farm were from an arm. Barbara Galbraith reckoned that Melissa Jordan dropped the other leg down a bore hole, or something similar, on the moors near Osmotherley. We need to get a confirmation from Melissa, and to take us to the site she used. She's lived in Osmotherley for years, hasn't she, so she ought to know the area pretty well. That leaves us with the missing arm, which Galbraith reckoned her husband hid down a drain somewhere."

"I think she's lying, Sir," Sharpe suggested, "because he could have just dumped it overboard like the torso. I bet she hid it somewhere near to where they lived in Whitby."

"Maybe," Bentley continued, "after all, they all agreed to dispose of one body part each. We'll have to keep working on her. George, you can help out there, and you'll need some kind of statement from Amelia. I guess a sworn statement involving her mother would be acceptable?" He looked around the room. "As I said before, we've still got plenty to do. I'll organise a press conference here for later this afternoon. Debbie, you can front that one with me." She nodded.

"I think I'm right in saying that Phoebe Bartlett's father is still alive, Sir?" she said.

"That's true," Slater confirmed. "He still lives in Barnsley."

"Your wife's a relative, isn't she, Dennis. Why don't you take her to do a little shopping, and pop in to see Mr Jordan?"

"OK, Sir."

"Make sure that he's not in a home somewhere, with dementia, or something like that." Slater smiled. "I don't want to waste valuable funds on a trip to Debenham's."

"I can discuss some funeral arrangements with

him, Sir, that's if I can find out when her body will be released."

"That could be some time, Dennis, you know, as we've still got to find some of it." Bentley thought for a moment. "How about a memorial service for her?"

"Good idea, Sir, I'll see how he feels about that."

"Poor bastard," muttered Sharpe, "one daughter gets murdered and chopped up, and the other is going to be locked up for the rest of his life, and more."

"Right, I need a coffee. Is there anything else?" Chapman shook her head.

"I think we've got enough to do for now, Sir," she said. "Anyone else for a drink?" Sharpe raised a hand, the others nodded. "Good, you can sort them out, Sharpie!" Bentley moved to Ryan's desk.

"A quiet word in my office, George." Ryan got up, and followed the DI. "Take a seat, George. I just wanted to give you a pat on the back for your work on this case, son. I didn't want to say anything in front of the others, but your thinking has been brilliant, in a different league to the rest of us." Ryan began to protest. "Shut up, George, and listen to what I'm saying. We wouldn't have got this far without your little theories and hunches. You've noticed things that the rest of us have missed. I'm telling you now, George, you've got a great career ahead of you, but you need to start thinking about your future." Ryan listened carefully. "I'm advising you to put in for your sergeant's exams as soon as you can."

"I'm not sure if I'm ready for that, Sir, and I'm happy with the way things are going at the moment. I've still got a lot to learn."

"You never stop learning, George. Even an old git like me is still learning." Ryan smiled. "Look, George, I lost my son Brian years ago, and had he lived he would have been about the same age as you. If he was in your shoes, I'd be saying the same things to him. You need to look beyond Scarborough CID. Who knows, Debbie may move on, and there could be an opening here, but you don't get on well with Sharpe, do you?"

"I don't dislike him, Sir."

"Yeah, but he could be trouble if you got promoted above him, so look at the broader picture. There'll be other openings in North Yorkshire, or in another force. Listen, George, take a few days off, and take Fiona somewhere nice. Talk things over with her, and when you have, come and see me again. OK?" Ryan stood up. "They say Dublin's a nice city, George. Why don't you spend a few days there, and tell me all about it?" He grinned. "Who knows, you may bump into our Maddie!"

• PART FOUR •

CHAPTER THIRTY-TWO

George sat back as the waitress deposited an enormous bowl of stew on the table in front of him. Two large balls of potato were floating on the surface. “Wow!” he exclaimed, smiling as Fiona received a more modest portion of lamb cutlets. “I’ve had stew at home many times,” he said to the waitress, a long-dark-haired young woman, “but it never looked like this!”

“You’re in Dublin now, Sir,” she grinned, speaking with a broad Irish brogue, “this is proper Irish stew. Enjoy,” she added, as she moved away in the direction of the kitchen.

“Cheers,” George spoke to Fiona, raising his glass of Guinness. She clinked her glass of pinot grigio.

“Cheers, George,” she laughed softly, “you’re certainly going the whole hog on the Irish thing tonight!”

“Well, you know what they say, Fiona, when in Rome…”

"Whatever, but I have to admit, this trip to Dublin was a great suggestion from old Bentley."

"That's true," George replied, ladling a large dose of stew into his mouth, "I hadn't realised that Dublin would be so interesting. I mean, I've read something about the Easter Rising and the history of the Republic, but walking around the city and visiting Kilmainham Jail has brought it all to life."

"You should have been a history teacher, George."

"I did consider it briefly," he continued munching through his stew, as the waitress reappeared.

"Is everything alright for the both of you?" she asked.

"Lovely," Fiona replied, as George put up a thumb.

"Just shout me if you need anything else," she smiled widely.

"OK, thanks." Fiona chewed on a lamb cutlet. "So what made you join the police?"

"I'm not sure really, Fi, I guess I didn't fancy dealing with the unruly kids in the "C" classes."

"I think you'd have made a good teacher, George, after all, you've managed to get me interested in history. I can't wait to visit the next museum," she added, with a cheeky grin on her face.

"Yeah, right." He carried on digging into his bowl. "It's our last day tomorrow, Fi, so what do you fancy doing?" He chewed another mouthful, as she finished her meal. "Your choice."

"Well, I was thinking of a nice romantic evening

tonight, followed by some shopping therapy tomorrow." She glanced at his bowl. "I guess the romance is out of the window … you'll struggle to get onto the bed after eating that lot!" They both laughed. "The shopping is still on though. I'll lead the way this time."

***

George eased his car to a halt outside the large house in Scarborough which had been converted into flats. He looked across the road. "It's nice that Debbie's away tonight, Fiona, as it gives us another night together before we get back to reality tomorrow."

"Yes," she muttered, reaching for her handbag, "it would have been nice to stay away for longer, but … next time, eh?"

"I'll get the cases," George said, exiting the car and opening the boot. He lifted them out, then headed across the road, as Fiona was putting her coat over her arm. She followed him up the steps to the front door, then stopped.

"Blast! I've left my phone in the car. Pass me the car key, please, George," she said, rummaging in her handbag. "You go on up," she added, tossing him the keys for the flat. She returned to the car, found her mobile in the door tidy, then picked up a couple of magazines before locking the car. She opened the front door and headed up the stairs to the first floor, pushing open the door to Debbie's flat. The hallway was in darkness, but Fiona could see a low light from the lounge. She walked a few paces, pushed the door open slowly and smiled, muttering "How romantic!" Fiona took another step, then stopped suddenly, her coat and magazines tumbling to the floor.

"That's what I thought, Fiona," grinned Gary Henderson, sitting relaxed in an armchair, "how nice to see you again!"

CHAPTER THIRTY-THREE

"Gary, my God, what a shock!" Fiona steadied herself on the doorframe, and sensed that there was someone else behind her. She turned and saw two men in the shadows in the hallway. "Who are …?"

"Come in and sit down, Fiona," Henderson stood up and gestured to the two men to go away. One of them closed the door, as Henderson guided her to the settee. "I thought this would be a nice surprise for you."

"No, it's not," she exclaimed, placing her hand on her forehead. "Oh, my God, where's …?"

"Your friend? Don't worry about him, Fiona, my lads have taken care of him."

"But …"

"Forget about him, love, it's just about you and me now … remember, like we discussed every time you came to visit me in Strangeways? You knew that I had been released, didn't you?"

"On parole, yes."

"Well, as you'll see later, we can forget about that parole. I've got everything arranged, Fiona, and it doesn't involve parole, believe me. I've done enough time, and now that's history. "We've got a great …"

"I want to know what you've done with George?"

"Relax, baby, as I said before, the lads are looking after him." Fiona looked terrified. "Look, there's nothing to worry about, they haven't killed him … yet."

"He's got nothing to do with you and me, Gary. If you harm a hair on his head, we're over, and you can forget about all the arrangements you have made."

"Look, Fiona," he smiled widely, and she gazed into his deep-blue eyes, "your friend … George, yes, well he's alright, and I promise you that nothing bad will happen to him, just as long as everything goes as planned. Understand?"

"What plans, Gary?"

"Do you remember, Fiona, it must be five years ago, just before my trial, that I told you that I would never take revenge on you after you betrayed me to the police? I promised you then that I had forgiven you … that I totally understood why you had grassed on me, but that when I was released, I would make everything up to you. Do you remember all of that, Fiona, and how you promised that you would wait for me?"

"Yes, I remember those times we met, Gary, and what we said," she admitted quietly.

"Good, because nothing has changed for me, baby

… nothing at all. In fact, I told you not to visit me again until I had been released, remember? I wanted you to have some normality, and to enjoy life until we could be together again." He laughed. "I never thought that you'd join the bloody police, mind!"

"So you know about my life now?"

"Most of it, Fiona, enough to think that we can have a good future together, well away from this stinking country."

"Look, I'm worried about …" She sat upright on the settee, but Henderson placed a hand on her shoulder and opened the door.

"Wingnut!" he shouted, and two figures emerged from the kitchen. He spoke to them in whispers. "She wants to know about the bloke."

"He's in the hall cupboard," the taller of the two men answered.

"Yes, he's fine," Woodend smiled, "just a bit tied up for now … well, taped up."

"Still alive?" Woodend opened the cupboard, and checked the body crammed into the bottom corner.

"He's bleeding a bit, but still breathing. He's out for the count, Gary, but he'll be OK."

"Right, I shouldn't be too long, but don't get pissed. We've a long drive ahead of us." The other man nodded, and he and Woodend returned to the kitchen. Henderson moved back into the lounge. "He's alright, Fiona, he'll be fine … honest."

"I want to see him."

"You don't believe me? Come on, love, we go back a long way, and you can trust me on this." She stood up. "OK, you can see him later. We've still got things to discuss, and time is running out." They both sat down on the settee, and he put his arm around her, touching her long blonde hair. "I've missed you, Fiona, really missed you. We were great together, weren't we?"

"Until your drugs killed my best friend," she replied angrily.

"I know, and I'm really sorry about that, I fucked things up, but I meant what I told you years ago, that I've finished with drugs forever, and that we've got a great future together."

"A great future together … where, Gary?"

"In southern Spain."

"Southern Spain, Gary, what do you mean … the Costa del Crime?"

"Well, there probably are some criminals living there, Fiona, but you grew up in Liverpool, for Christ's sake. You've been surrounded by criminals all of your life."

"Yes, and I'm looking at one of them." *I need to keep him talking, to keep him sweet and get out of here, to give George some more time!*

"I told you before, Fiona, and I mean it, I am going straight. Everything is arranged, and we'll have a great life together in Spain. My mother has invested a lot of my money, baby, and we've a beautiful villa, a bar and some shops waiting for us out there. I've also got a block of flats that's almost built. That's our future", he smiled, "and it's all ours, all paid for and all totally legit."

"Not quite, Gary, you're breaking your parole." *God, those eyes. I wish he'd stop looking at me like that,* she thought, trying to resist his sexual attraction. "Interpol will be on our back for the rest of our lives, or until you're caught again."

"I'm not that stupid, Fiona, I've got new identities for both of us … passports and everything, and all of the documents relating to my property, as well as the rest of my cash, are all deposited in an offshore account. The police won't be able to trace it back to me." He grinned, and hugged her. "You see, my love, I've thought of everything, even down to the flight bookings for early tomorrow morning."

"What if I refuse to go with you, Gary … what then?"

"I didn't even consider it, Fiona. Come on, how many times did we discuss our future once I had been released? I made that promise to you to sort everything out, and I've kept it. Nothing has changed for me, so what are you saying, Fiona," he spoke angrily, pointing outside the door, "is he the problem?"

"Oh no, Gary," she gripped his arm, "he means nothing to me, but I'm worried that you might harm him, and he's a policeman. We've got to take a lot of risks as it is, you know, searching for the great future you've planned for us, without injuring a policeman ..."

"Or worse," Henderson spoke the words she was thinking. "I've told you, Fiona, he's OK, and no harm will come to him as long as everything goes well with us. Is that clear enough for you?" He smiled again, and relaxed back on the settee.

"I suppose so, but I'm risking everything by fleeing abroad with you. You better hadn't let me down, Gary."

"You've nothing to fear, Fiona. I've got it all sorted." *Those blue eyes again!*

"OK, so if I agree to come with you, Gary, what's next?"

"There's not a lot to do, babe, but we haven't got much time left. You need to throw a few things into a small suitcase …"

"A few things, Gary," she gasped, "but I've got loads of clothes that I need to take with me, many of them favourite things, you know."

"Forget them, Fiona, we'll buy new after we get to Spain. After all, you won't need all of those heavy coats and woolly knickers, will you?" he grinned. "No, just a few basics, that's all you need for now, plus your toiletries and anything sentimental that you can't live without."

"Christ, Gary," she muttered, running her hands through her hair, "a life-changing trip, and you said we haven't much time."

"That's right, Fi, we need to go as soon as you're ready. We've got close to a three-hour drive to Manchester Airport before checking in for your flight. Oh, and dress casually, babe. Fasten your hair into a bun or something like that, and wear a woolly hat, plus sunglasses. I don't want you looking gorgeous until we get to Spain."

"Right," she said anxiously, "and I'll have to find my passport."

"You won't need that … I've got you a new one."

"So who am I now?"

"I'll tell you at the airport, so come on, get a move on!" He followed her out of the lounge into her bedroom, watched her open a small case on the bed, then headed into the kitchen. "Shouldn't be too long now, lads," he told the others. "Grab a few snacks for the journey, just in case we get delayed somewhere." He moved back into the hallway and glanced in the bedroom, where Fiona was packing some clothes and a washbag into the suitcase she had used for the Dublin trip. Henderson returned to the kitchen.

"What about the guy in the cupboard?" asked the taller man.

"Did you hit him hard, Kev?"

"Too right, gave him a hell of a clout. He won't wake up until the morning, and you'll be well on your way by then."

"I didn't want to leave any complications behind," Henderson muttered, "but Fiona said he's a copper."

"Best not kill the fucker, Gary," Woodend advised, "you don't want the police chasing you all around Europe."

"I could leave one of you here to make sure that he doesn't complicate matters."

"Yes, but what if something goes wrong, you know, if that other policewoman comes back suddenly?"

"Can't you handle a woman, Wingnut?"

"'Course I can," Woodend replied, offended.

"Don't worry, Chris, you're probably right. I don't want either of you to be caught here, then start singing to the police. That could fuck up everything for me out in Spain." Fiona appeared at the bedroom doorway, her blonde locks piled into a bun.

"I just need some perfume, and women's stuff, you know." Woodend grinned.

"Hurry up then, love," Henderson glanced at his watch, "it's time we were leaving." He watched her enter the bathroom, then turned to Kev. "Check that bloke again, Kev." The taller man lifted the catch on the cupboard, and knelt down.

"Still out for the count, Gary, but still breathing." He closed the door and dropped the catch, then Fiona joined them, clutching a toiletries bag.

"All done," she smiled at Henderson. "Ready to go." She selected a coat from the hall, put in on, and Woodend went around, switching off the lights. All was quiet as they descended the stairs, opened the front door, and walked down the street to Henderson's blue Mercedes.

"I've not long had this motor," he smiled at Fiona, "and I'll miss her."

"Just like my clothes, Gary, so no doubt you'll buy another in Spain," she replied frostily. Henderson opened the boot, placed Fiona's case inside, then they all got inside the car. He switched on the engine, then Fiona gasped. "Shit, Gary, I've forgotten my tablets."

"Tablets, what tablets?"

"Amlopidine, Gary, I've got high blood pressure, and I've got to take them without fail every day. Any stress, you know, could …"

"Alright, alright," Henderson snapped, "where the fuck are they?"

"In the bathroom cabinet, Gary, I'll only be a minute."

"Go on, hurry up!" Henderson muttered anxiously. "Kev, Wingnut, you can both go with her, and don't take your eyes off her, right?" They got out of the car and walked alongside Fiona as she returned to the flat. They made their way quietly up the stairs and Fiona opened the door and went in the flat, followed by Woodend. Kev waited outside the door. Fiona moved to the bathroom, flicked on the light, and stepped outside a minute later, clutching a bottle of tablets.

"Got them!" she said softly, switching off the light and following Woodend to the door. As she did so, in the darkness, she flicked up the catch on the cupboard, then the three of them left the building.

At least he has a chance, she thought as she walked with the others back to the car.

***

The 110-mile journey from York to the M60, the extensive ring-road around Manchester, was uneventful. Henderson did all of the driving and Fiona, sitting in the passenger seat, had pretended to sleep for much of the way. Woodend stayed awake all of the time, but Kev Langton, sitting in the back behind Fiona, kept on dozing off and snoring loudly. Henderson pulled in to the Hartshead Services on the M62, and sat with Fiona while the other two went to the toilet, and brought some takeaway drinks and pastries back to the car. All four then escorted Fiona to the services, and watched and waited until she had finished in the toilets, and was ready to return to the car.

"You don't trust me much, do you, Gary?" she asked in the car park.

"It's not that, Fiona, it's just that I've got a hell of a lot riding on this trip, and I don't want anything to go wrong and jeopardise our future in Spain. That's why I've got my babysitters with me." He smiled in the darkness. "I do trust you, babe, and I still love you very much. Think about it, why else would I be taking all of these risks?"

"I could have tried to escape in Scarborough, Gary, so give me a bit of credit. If I didn't love you so much, I wouldn't be here on this crazy adventure with you, would I?" He laughed.

"Just wait until you're sunning yourself on the poolside in my villa, Fiona, then you'll thank me for all of this!" He kissed her passionately, put his arm around her, and they stumbled along to the car, closely followed by Langton and Woodend, who was eating another pastry.

***

George Ryan blinked slowly, then opened his eyes. He was in total darkness, and he had a thumping headache. He tried to raise his hand to touch his head, but quickly realised that both hands were fastened securely behind his back. Breathing heavily, George attempted to move, but his feet were taped together as well, and he seemed to be jammed into a hole. His body ached all over, and as he tried to move slightly, he bumped his head on a shelf, and cried out in pain. George lay still, and tried to remember his last movements. Fiona's flat! They had returned from the break in Dublin, and she went back to his car for something, leaving him to open the door to the flat. After that, nothing! George tried to ignore the throbbing pain on the back of his head, and attempted to ease himself into a sitting position. Gradually, the stiffness lessened, and he moved his legs slowly up and down, and inched his body upwards. Twisting to his left, he leant against the cupboard door and tumbled out onto the hallway carpet, crying out in muffled pain as his head touched the floor. He lay still for a few minutes, closing his eyes, then opened them again and twisted from one side to another, trying to get his bearings.

A pale light filtered through to the hallway from Fiona's bedroom, and George eased himself up against a wall, thinking furiously of ways in which he could release himself, or summon up some help. If burglars were involved here, it was possible that Fiona was tied up in another room, but why hadn't they both been placed in the cupboard, and why had the door been left open? George thought back to the red car he had seen parked in the street, and a more sinister scenario entered his head. Henderson! It had to have something to do with him. George had been tied up to give Henderson some time, but time to do what? To kidnap Fiona, or worse, to kill her … to take his revenge. Whatever the motive, George needed to free himself and get help fast.

He began to wriggle his way to the kitchen, thinking that if he could find a knife and drop it onto the floor, he might be able to cut the tape which was binding his hands and legs. Gradually he edged his way to the kitchen doorway, where he managed to get into a sitting position, then painfully to shuffle his body up the wall. He hopped into the kitchen, located the light switch on the wall, and, banging it with his nose several times, finally switched on the light. Breathing heavily, he glanced around the kitchen, but there wasn't a knife in sight. He hopped again towards the drawers, and biting hard through the tape covering his mouth, George finally managed to ease the top drawer open. He could see the knives, forks, spoons and so on neatly stacked in their individual recesses, but no amount of barging with his shoulder could release any of them. After many minutes of frustrated effort, George stood still and thought again.

He hopped slowly back into the hallway, then made his way into the lounge. His head was throbbing madly by now. George searched for the light switch, and another few minutes of banging it with his nose filled the room with light. He looked around for the TV remote, spotting it on the coffee table. He knelt down, banged his nose on the red "ON" switch, then looked for the volume controls. A shopping channel filled the TV screen. George located the "+" button, and kept his nose pressed down on it until the TV reached full volume. He sat back against the settee, exhausted by his efforts, and with the pain on the back of his head getting stronger by the minute. *Come on, wake up somebody!* He closed his eyes, and waited.

After what seemed to be hours, there was some furious banging on the door. "Debbie, Fiona, are you alright?" More banging, then George heard another person speaking. "Where's the spare key, Graham?" A minute or two passed, then the door opened and four people, all wearing dressing gowns, piled into the flat and found George in the lounge. One of the women rushed into the kitchen, and returned with some scissors, cutting George's tapes and freeing his hands and feet. The older man switched off the TV, as George eased the tape from his mouth.

"Thank you," he smiled at her, rubbing his arms and legs, and easing himself onto the settee.

"You're bleeding," the other woman said, and both of the women went into the kitchen to look for a first aid kit.

"You're Fiona's friend, aren't you?" the other man asked, as the women returned with some cotton wool and a bowl of warm water. The younger one began bathing the wound on the back of George's head, as he replied to the question.

"Yes, I'm George Ryan, a policeman," he answered, wincing as the woman attended to his wound.

"Where's Debbie and Fiona?"

"Debbie's in Leeds, but Fiona was with me last night when we returned here from Dublin. Somebody must have been waiting for us, and they've clobbered me and taken Fiona. There's no time to lose," he gasped anxiously, "please phone the police as quickly as you can." He fainted onto the settee.

***

Gary Henderson indicated left and turned off the M62 at its junction with the A627, heading for Oldham, and beyond, for Manchester Airport. It was still dark, just after three-thirty in the morning, and it was drizzling slightly, but there was a lot of traffic on the roads, even at this early hour. Fiona roused as the car slowed down, smiled at Henderson, then glanced behind her, where Langton was still snoring, more lightly now. Chris Woodend was wide awake, and he laughed softly. "Sleeping Beauty! Feel better now?"

"Give it a rest," Henderson said gruffly. "I need you to keep an eye on the road signs, Chris, just to make sure that we're heading in the right direction."

“It’s easy, Gary, just skirt around Oldham and head for Stockport. You’ll pick up the airport signs before too long.” Henderson nodded, glanced at Fiona, then began to pick up speed.

“Not too far now, babe.” Fiona closed her eyes again, and settled back in her seat. Henderson overtook a couple of heavy trucks, then as he drove around a long bend, he noticed that the traffic was slowing up ahead of him. “Bloody traffic lights,” he muttered to himself as he applied the brakes and came to a halt behind two more wagons. Quick as a flash, Fiona opened the passenger door and darted out onto the road, running alongside the wagons. “Wingnut, quick, get after her!” he shouted loudly, and Woodend exited the car and ran by the wagons in pursuit. “Langton!” Henderson bellowed, “fucking wake up and get after them!”

Fiona raced past the wagons, which were still waiting for the lights to change, glanced behind her at the nearing Woodend, then gripped the bonnet of the front wagon and swung herself right, before dashing in front of it, heading for the empty outside lane. She screamed as another truck, turning right on the filter lane, narrowly avoided her as she raced across the road, but there was no hope for Woodend, close behind now, who was clattered by the wagon and sent flying through the air, his arms and legs flailing wildly, and across the dual carriageway, to fall in a crumpled heap on the roadside. Fiona carried on running for her life, glancing behind her to see the ambling figure of Langton thirty yards behind her. The lights changed, and Henderson swung his car into the filter lane, searching for the fleeing figure in the darkness. He passed Langton who pointed as Fiona turned right down a side road, still running strongly. Henderson drove past the big man, screamed his car right and put his lights on full beam, spotting the flowing locks of Fiona as she continued running. He put his foot down hard, grinning as he neared her, then she stopped suddenly, stared briefly at the car and walked straight out in front of it.

***

Don Bentley and Debbie Chapman spoke quietly to the ward sister at the nurses' station, then made their way along the corridor, looking for the side ward, where George Ryan lay in bed, his head heavily bandaged. Bentley moved two chairs closer to the bed, and they sat down, waiting for Ryan to wake up. An auxiliary nurse pushed a trolley noisily past the room, and Ryan stirred, part-opened his eyes, then tried to sit up against the pillow.

"Easy, George," Bentley smiled, getting up to support him, "take it easy, young fellow … you've been in the wars." He sat down, as Debbie Chapman looked out of the window.

"Hello, Sir, Debbie," he muttered drowsily, "how long have you been sitting there?"

"Not too long, George," Bentley answered. "Would you like a drink?"

"No, thank you, I'm fine for now," he winced,

then smiled briefly. "I've got a rotten headache." Ryan looked at Chapman. "You're quiet, Debbie, it's not …" he began, then stared at Bentley. "Last night, Sir, after Fiona and I returned," he paused, "someone broke into your flat, Debbie, and … where's Fiona, Sir?"

"There's no easy way to tell you, George," Bentley began, as Debbie Chapman started sobbing, "Fiona died last night in a road accident."

"A road accident, Fiona dead?" Ryan asked in disbelief. "Where?"

"It happened near Oldham, George. Are you alright, son?" he paused, standing up to grip Ryan's arm.

"It was Henderson, Sir," Ryan stated angrily, "Gary bloody Henderson, wasn't it?"

"It looks that way, George. He and another man, Chris Woodend … and maybe more, must have taken her when you returned to Debbie's flat. We have a lorry driver witness, and he told Manchester Police that he was waiting at some lights when a blonde woman darted out of a car and ran into the road. Two men chased her, and one of them, Woodend, was struck by a wagon and killed. A Mercedes drove after the woman and the other man, and turned off onto a side road. That's where the police found Fiona's body. She'd been hit by a car." Bentley glanced at Debbie Chapman. "I'm really sorry, George, but she was already dead by the time the ambulance arrived." Ryan sat with his head in his hands, shaking and tearful.

"Fiona … I can't believe it, Debbie." She moved to Ryan's bed and put her arms around him, and they both cried together … one for a friend, the other for a lover.

***

Later that morning, Ryan spoke more rationally with Bentley. "Henderson, Sir, did they find any trace of him?"

"No, George, he must have been planning this for a long time, and we think that he and the other man carried on to Manchester Airport, where Henderson had a flight booked. We know that Fiona visited Henderson in Strangeways for a couple of years after he was put away, so perhaps they had always planned to escape abroad once he had been released on parole."

"That might have been the case at first, Sir, but then she looked for a different life, moving away from Liverpool and joining North Yorkshire Police. She loved living over here, Sir." He paused, glancing out of the window. "I loved her, Sir," he muttered softly, tears forming in his eyes, "she was a beautiful woman." Bentley nodded. "Fiona was frightened of Henderson, Sir, but recently, we'd grown so close and I don't think she was frightened anymore." He thought for a moment. "She may have gone off with him willingly last night, Sir, but I can tell you this for certain. She did it to save my life … and now it's cost hers."

CHAPTER THIRTY-FOUR

Gary Henderson took a sip of his latte, then continued reading his copy of the Daily Mirror. It was a warm, sunny day, and he had selected a shady table outside a café just off the promenade at Benalmadina, on the coast of Andalusia. During the short time he had been in southern Spain, Henderson had kept a low profile, visiting the town only to buy a newspaper and enjoy a coffee before returning to his villa on the outskirts of the resort. He was yet to visit his bar and shops in nearby Torremolinos, but he had walked past his block of apartments close to the promenade in the town, which were nearing completion. He flicked a page, had another drink and glanced along the street. A tall, long-haired blonde, pulling a medium-sized pink suitcase behind her, was approaching the café. The young woman, wearing tight-fitting jeans and top, halted, wiped her brow, then selected a table just a few feet away from Henderson. Henderson admired her figure for a few seconds, then continued reading his paper as she ordered a coke from the waiter, and looked up and down the street as she waited for her drink. She glanced in Henderson's direction and he looked up, smiled at her, then carried on with his reading. The glass of coke arrived, and as Henderson turned another page, he noticed that she was smiling at him. He removed his sunglasses, and returned the smile, brushing his fingers through his dyed dark hair. "Have you just arrived here?" he asked, putting his newspaper on the table and smiling widely again.

"Yes, this is my first day here," she replied in a strong eastern European accent, before taking a sip of her drink. "I hope to find work here," she added.

"Do you mind if I join you?" Henderson asked, standing up. She gestured at the empty chair next to her, and he moved across and sat down. "Thanks," he smiled, "my name's Gary."

"I am called Alexandra," she smiled, "but my friends call me Sasha."

"That's a nice name," he said, grinning, "so I shall call you Sasha." She blushed, and took another sip of her coke. "Your accent … where are you from, Sasha?"

"I am from Belarus." He looked puzzled. "It is near Russia." They laughed.

"Ah, I thought you sounded foreign," he muttered, then added quickly, "but your English is very good, Sasha."

"Thank you, and you are …?"

"I'm English, Sasha, from a city called Liverpool."

"I have heard of this city, Gary, maybe football?"

"Good girl," Henderson said proudly, "Liverpool Football Club, "the Reds", and The Beatles, they came from Liverpool as well."

"Beetles?" she replied, frowning and looking at the ground. "I don't understand."

"Of course," Henderson grinned, "you're too young, Sasha. The Beatles were a music band … a long time ago." She finished her drink.

"Would you like another?"

"You are very kind, Gary, but I need to find a cheap hotel where I can stay, then I have to find a job." Henderson thought for a moment.

"Look, Sasha, I live on the outskirts of Benalmadina … not too far away. Why don't you come back to my villa, where you can have a shower and get changed, you know, freshen up? After that, I can show you some of the hotels, and perhaps help you to find some work." She gazed into his deep-blue eyes.

"You are very kind, Gary."

***

Sasha moaned more loudly and buried her face into Henderson's shoulder as he climaxed, and his thrusting movements gradually slowed down. He eased himself off her, and moved onto his side, smiling then kissing her passionately. She touched the sweat on his forehead and chest, then he ran his fingers down her face, coaxing her blonde hair onto her shoulder and gently caressing her right breast. They kissed again and laughed softly, before embracing each other firmly. They parted, and Sasha, blushing a little, pulled up the sheet to cover her body. She glanced around the room, then looked into Henderson's eyes. "I thought you were going to show me your house!" They both laughed loudly.

"We've plenty of time for that, Sasha," Henderson whispered, then kissed her again. "Would you like a drink?" She nodded, and he eased himself off the bed and headed out of the room, returning a minute or two later with two glasses of coke. Sasha was sitting up against the pillow, and the sheet had dropped to expose her full breasts. "You're beautiful," he grinned, passing her one of the glasses, before taking a gulp himself. He sat down on the bed next to her, and she ran her hand along his naked left thigh. Henderson drained his glass and placed it on the bedside table. "What kind of work are you looking for, Sasha?"

"I would like to work in a bar, or a restaurant," she replied, sipping her drink, "or maybe in a hotel. I don't mind, Gary, because just now, I need to work to earn some money. I would like a job where I can meet other people," she continued in her strong accent. "I like people," she added, smiling. Henderson looked at her face, then her breasts.

"Yeah, and I think people will like you, Sasha!" They both laughed again. "You're a great-looking girl." He lifted the sheet and slid back next to her, pulling her gently towards him. He thought for a few minutes. "Sasha, I've only been here for a short time. I had to sort out a lot of things in England, before I could move my business interests out here." She eased away from him slightly, listening carefully. "This villa is mine, and I will need someone to look after it, but I also have a bar and some shops in Torremolinos … a small town not too far away. People are looking after them for me there already, but I like to choose my own people to work for me. That will take some time, but I may be able to offer you some work, Sasha. We can check things over together, then you can decide if you would like to work with me." He paused, caressing her again. "What do you think?"

"It is a nice idea, Gary," she replied seriously, "but what if you decide that you don't like me, or that I don't enjoy working for you … what then? After all, we have just met each other."

"You're a sensible girl, Sasha. Look, I have a proposition for you. Stay here for as long as you want, have a look at my businesses with me, and use my villa as a base for looking around for other work in Benalmadina. It won't cost you anything, and if you find something else, or someone else that you prefer … fine! You can take your time, there's no hurry."

"You are very kind, Gary, thank you. It's a nice idea, but are you sure?"

"Definitely, Sasha."

"OK, then I will accept your offer." She leant over and kissed him. "Now, are you going to show me the rest of your villa?"

“Later, baby,” he muttered, kissing her more passionately and shifting the sheet down the bed. She moved her hand down his body, and smiled as he quickly became aroused. “Later.”

CHAPTER THIRTY-FIVE

Friday, the second of March. George Ryan looked in the mirror to make sure that his black tie was fastened properly, and straightened his suit jacket. He flicked open the curtain to check on the weather. Cloudy, but not raining ... yet. He had a final glance in the mirror, then opened the door and knocked on Debbie Chapman's room next door. She poked her head around the door a few seconds later. "Christ, George! Give me a few more minutes, no, make that ten minutes. There'll still be something downstairs to eat for breakfast, so stop flapping, will you? Ten minutes, at least, OK?" She slammed the door.

George and Debbie had travelled from Scarborough on Thursday morning, taking their time and arriving in Liverpool mid-afternoon. He had done most of the driving, and Debbie navigated him to the neat semi-detached house in Aintree, where Fiona's parents lived. They had spent just over an hour with the couple, who looked to be a similar age to Don Bentley. There were a few tears, but Fiona's parents seemed grateful that George and Debbie had taken the time to share some of their recent memories of Fiona with them. "Fiona was happy in Yorkshire," her mother had said, "very happy." She had looked at George and added: "I wish she had met you years ago, George, instead of that monster Henderson. He ruined her life, and now she's paid the final price." This brought about another flood of tears.

Now George and Debbie planned to have breakfast in their hotel, before driving the short distance to St Giles Parish Church in Aintree, where the funeral service was due to begin at ten o-clock. George sat on his bed, and reflected on his time with Fiona … good times and now, bad times … but mostly it had been good times, and George had found real love. He closed his eyes, and could picture her beautiful face, her lovely blonde hair, her good sense of humour … everything he liked about her. If only, he reprimanded himself, if only I had taken more positive action over that car in the street, then …? Now he would never know. He wiped a tear from his eye, and went into the bathroom to wash his face. He finished drying himself and gargled a little mouthwash, then Debbie knocked firmly on the door. "Ready, George?" she muttered, as he opened the door.

"I suppose so, Debbie. But I don't feel very hungry."

"Best to eat something, son," she smiled and put her arm around him. "Be strong, George," she advised him, "in our line of work you have to get used to this sort of thing."

"Maybe, but Fiona was not *this sort of thing*. She was special, Debbie." He breathed in deeply, and they walked along the corridor together.

***

"Good Morning, Sir," Tim Sharpe smiled as Don Bentley entered the Incident Room. The stocky DI nodded, and wandered over to the front desk. "It feels a bit weird in here today, Sir, you know, just the two of us."

"I feel OK, Tim," Bentley joked, "if there's anything weird in here, it's you." Sharpe laughed. "What are you on with?"

"Reports, Sir, just writing up reports … I've got loads to do." He touched a small heap of papers on his desk. "Have you heard from Debbie?"

"No, but I don't expect to." He glanced at his watch. "Nine-thirty. They'll be gathering for the funeral." Sharpe looked up. "It's due at ten."

"It's a sad day, Sir," Sharpe muttered with feeling. "Dennis away as well?"

"Yes, he and his missus are going to see Phoebe Bartlett's father this morning."

"I wouldn't like to be in his shoes, Sir, one daughter brutally murdered, the other banged up for taking part in it."

"True, and he must be getting on a bit. Melissa's over fifty, isn't she?"

"I think so. What time's the service in Barnsley?"

"Two-thirty. I can't see many people being there, Tim. Her family and friends up here are dead or locked up, and there may not be too many relatives near Barnsley."

"No, but there'll be a few nosey gits, you know, after all she was the local glamour girl, wasn't she?"

"Yes, and the press will be there. It's a good story for them." He thought for a moment. "Right, got to move on." He headed for his office.

"Fancy a coffee before we get to work?"

"Aye, go on," Bentley called from his office. "Don't forget the bloody sugar this time." Sharpe grinned, and shuffled down the corridor as Bentley's phone rang. "Hello." He listened for a minute or so, then answered enthusiastically. "Christ, Jean, that's great news." Another pause. "Now listen, love, wait until I get home, OK?" He listened again intently. "Too right, Jean, this is fantastic news. I'll see you later, love." He put the phone down, then Sharpe appeared in the doorway, holding two steaming mugs.

"I could hear your voice down the corridor, Sir, and now you look as happy as a dog with two dicks." Bentley laughed. "What's the big news?" He placed a mug on Bentley's desk.

"We've had a letter from our Maddie, from Dublin, and this time she's written their phone number at the top," he said, beaming. "We still don't know where she lives, but at least we can call her and speak to her and the family, I hope."

"She's probably being cautious, Boss, just in case you give her a hard time."

"There's been a lot of water under the bridge since she left, Tim, and all we want is to get to know our daughter again, and to meet her family. That's all. The time for fighting is over, and we just want to be a family again." Sharpe smiled.

"I would have argued with you over that one not too long ago, but since having little Jasmine, I understand what you're saying. Families are important, Sir."

"Welcome to the human race, Sharpie," Bentley smirked. "I don't know how long this is going to last, but it's good to see."

"It's Jasmine's christening on Sunday, and there'll be loads of people there. I'm honestly looking forward to it," he smiled. "I'm going to get hammered."

"Huh, I thought your transformation was too good to be true, lad, but at least we've both got something to look forward to this weekend," Bentley said philosophically, "unlike the others. That's life, I suppose."

***

Gary Henderson eased his grip on Sasha's shoulders as their frantic session of lovemaking slowed down and stopped. He moved to one side, smiled at Sasha and watched her breasts rise and fall as her breathing returned to normal. She slid off the bed and headed for the bathroom. "I'm going to have a shower,

Gary. Will you make a drink for me, please?"

"Sure, babe, I'll be outside on the patio." He pulled on a pair of shorts, looked at his watch, and made his way to the kitchen. He poured two glasses of orange juice and grabbed a pain au chocolat from the kitchen, then opened the sliding door and ambled outside, squinting in the morning sunshine. Henderson dumped the glasses on the patio table, and, pastry in his mouth, walked back to the lounge, returning to the patio holding a newspaper. He sat down with his back to the sun, glanced at his watch again, took another bite out of the pain au chocolat, and opened the paper. It was yesterday's edition, and he searched for the story which had caught his eye the day before.

FUNERAL OF MURDERED POLICEWOMAN TOMORROW

The funeral of murdered policewoman Fiona Charlton will take place at St Giles' Church, Aintree, Liverpool tomorrow morning at 10 o'clock. Hundreds of mourners are expected to attend.

Miss Charlton died after being knocked down by a car driven by her former boyfriend, Gary Henderson, a convicted drugs dealer, who is believed to have fled to Spain.....

Henderson paused and sipped his drink. He looked at his watch again. Nearly eleven o'clock, but ten o'clock in the UK. Almost time for her funeral. He thought about the few days he had spent with Sasha, and smiled to himself, then about his relationship with Fiona. He looked at her photo in the newspaper article. *Bitch! She betrayed me twice, and now it's almost over. She deserved everything she got.* A shadow fell on the newspaper on the table, and he turned slightly, squinting in the strong morning sunshine. "Sasha …?"

"No, Gary," said a gruff voice, "sorry pal, … but there's no room for a cop-killer over here," and the heavy man raised his gun and pointed it at Henderson's chest as he turned towards him. The gun coughed and Henderson arched backwards, a ragged red hole appearing in his body as he sent the chairs and the table scattering across the patio. The man moved forward and knelt slightly, before firing a second shot at Henderson's head, taking off part of his temple in a blur of bloody gore. The man stood up and looked back at the sliding doors, where the young blonde woman was standing, her pink suitcase behind her.

"Are you done?" she asked in a heavy Scouse accent.

"All finished, Jess," he replied, "have you got everything?"

"Yes, I've got his passport, credit cards, and all of his money and papers that I could lay my hands on, and my bag's packed," she added, pointing to the suitcase. She moved forward and stared at the bloody corpse lying near the edge of the pool, a widening red circle staining the white tiles. "It's a pity, you know, he was so good-looking, and a great shag in bed." The man looked at her with distaste.

"Fucking scum," he muttered angrily, kicking Henderson's body until it rolled into the pool, slowly turning the water purple. "We're nicely set up here, and don't want the police poking into our business, causing unwanted trouble." He spat into the pool. "And as for him, Jess, well half the human population has a dick between it's legs, so it won't be long before you find another pretty boy." Jess laughed, and picked up her suitcase.

"Come on," she called, turning to leave, "it's time we got out of here."

***

We now commit Fiona's body to be cremated. We lovingly return her body to the elements from which it came. Ashes to ashes, dust to dust ....

George Ryan closed his eyes and switched off as the final prayers were being recited, and thought back to other elements of the service – the arrival of Fiona's coffin, the waiting crowds outside, the hymns and prayers, the eulogy delivered by one of Fiona's school friends – then he watched as the vicar recited a traditional Irish blessing, paused, as the pallbearers moved forward to lift Fiona's coffin onto their shoulders and slowly made their way along the aisle. Her parents and relatives, weeping and supporting each other, then slowly filed behind the coffin, and pew by pew, the church gradually emptied.

George and Debbie gave their final condolences to Fiona's parents outside the church. It was a chilly day, with a threat of rain, but Debbie had told them that she and George would be leaving after the church service, and would not go to the crematorium at Anfield. They had a lengthy drive ahead of them, she had explained, and she needed to call in at Northway to collect a few things for the weekend. George hadn't thought beyond the church service.

They stood just outside the main gate waiting for the hearse to leave, Debbie with tears in her eyes, George just numb. He stared at the large floral tribute "FIONA" alongside her coffin. At last, everyone was ready, and the hearse slowly drove off down the road, followed by cars full of family mourners and friends. George watched until the final cars were out of sight, then he loosened his tie. "Are you alright, George?" Debbie asked, touching his arm.

"I'm fine, Debbie, or at least I will be once we get on our way." He looked back at the church, then turned to her again. "I was just thinking over these past few weeks, Debbie. Life is full of secrets: Phoebe Bartlett with her secret affairs and flings; her sister and close family with their plot to murder her and dispose of her body; Parkinson looking after his old mother, with a cannabis farm in his barns." He smiled briefly. *And you, Debbie, with your friend in Leeds,* he thought. *Is it another woman, or a married man?* "Then there's Fiona, with her secret pledges to Henderson." Tears formed in his eyes. "I'm not sure if I really knew her, Debbie."

"Listen, George," she rebuked him sternly, "Fiona loved you. OK, maybe she still had feelings for Henderson after he was locked up, but her life changed when she met you. When she was living at my flat, George, she never stopped talking about you … if you'd phoned, where you were going, what you'd done together. Her love grew for you steadily, and I can tell you this, she was really looking forward to a future with you." She smiled. "When she went away with Henderson at the end, she probably stopped them from killing you, and made sure that you could get out of that cupboard. Her actions showed that she would rather have died than go away with him." She paused. "Don't forget that, George. She loved you." He thought for a moment, nodded slowly, then they walked along the road to where George had parked their car earlier that morning.

The crowds had by now largely dispersed. Across the road, standing at the back of the thinning knots of local mourners and press who had come to watch the funeral, Liz Coward gazed as George made his way back to his car with Debbie. Slimmer, and dressed more elegantly, Liz, on George's advice, had returned to Manchester University to continue her studies, but George hadn't wanted them to split up. It was her demons which had forced her to leave Scarborough.[2] She still had nightmares about the time when she had worked for the drug baron Nathaniel White, and bitter regrets about her affair with Tim Sharpe. *The bastard!* He had taken advantage of her when she was at a very low ebb, when she should have remained strong, and faithful to George. She longed to cross the road, to speak to George, to console him, even to kiss him, but this was not the time, not the place.

Liz continued to watch George as she followed them slowly on her side of the road, stopping when George and Debbie reached their car. He glanced back suddenly, and Liz turned and looked into a nearby garden. When she glanced back, the car had gone. *No*, she smiled to herself, *this is not the right time, but there will be a right time for us in the future.* Liz smiled to herself, turned and walked back along the road.

---

2 See 'Snow Maiden' and 'The Golden Chrysanthemums'

ACKNOWLEDGEMENTS

Much of my inspiration for this book came from our many visits to the Whitby and Scarborough area, where we have friends and always look forward to the splendid fish and chips! For those of you who know and love this part of North Yorkshire, I hope you feel that the settings are authentic, even if the story is wholly fictitious.

I wish to thank Rebekah Mills-Strawson, one of my delightful ex-pupils, for the invaluable information she supplied about children who are deaf without speech, as they are known today. Many thanks also to Fiona Satterthwaite, the lovely mature model on the front cover, and to Holly Holden, the talented young girl with her sketchbook. The map and drawings are my own, and ought to have been much better! Apologies to our friends Judith and Robert Ventress, of Intake Farm, for including yet another grim farm in this story, and a big thank you goes to Russell Holden, for once again making a great job of putting this book together. Any factual errors are solely down to me.

Finally, I wish to thank my wonderful partner for having the patience of a saint; my dogs Honey, Skye and Coco for keeping me company during the long hours spent in writing this book; and thanks also to my family and friends for continuing to support me in my literary efforts.

ABOUT THE AUTHOR

Naomi Hudson is married with two daughters and four grandchildren. She lives in south Cumbria. Following a varied career in teaching and other pursuits, she began writing novels less than four years ago. She has written five Lakeland topographical books, and her first novel, *Bluebell*, a romantic quest, was published towards the end of 2015. Another, *Aphrodite's Curse*, a tale of seduction and murder, was published in 2016. Her third novel, *Snow Maiden*, a tale of romance, betrayal and violence, was published in 2017. *The Golden Chrysanthemums*, the search for a serial killer in Whitby, became available last year. *The Secret* is her fifth novel. All are set in Yorkshire.

Naomi's books are available on Amazon and on Kindle. The author may be contacted on Facebook under Naomi Hudson (Bluebell author), and more information may be had on the website:

www.varykinocollectables.co.uk

Snow
Maiden
A TALE OF LOVE, BETRAYAL
AND MURDER SET IN MOSCOW
AND SCARBOROUGH
CLASSIFIED
NAOMI HUDSON

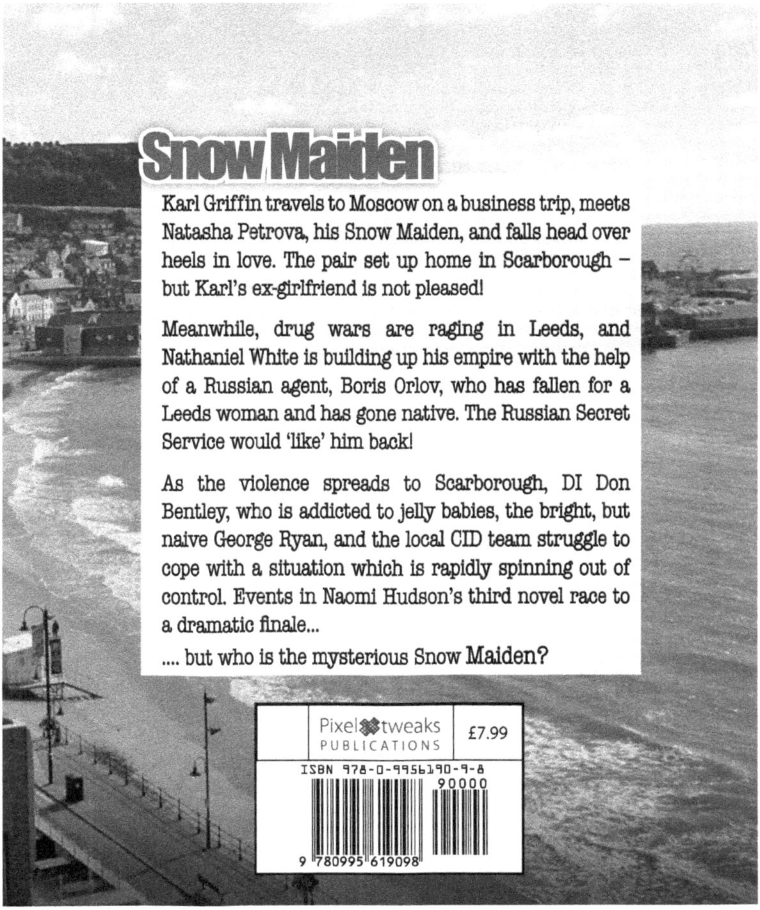

Paperback: 310 pages
Publisher: Varykino (17 Aug. 2017)
Language: English
ISBN: 978-0995619098
Product Dimensions: 12.7 x 1.8 x 20.3 cm

NAOMI HUDSON
the GOLDEN CHRYSANTHEMUMS
THE HUNT FOR A SERIAL KILLER IN WHITBY
a BENTLEY & RYAN THRILLER

Paperback: 280 pages

Publisher: Varykino (20 Feb. 2018)

Language: English

ISBN: 978-1999893675

Product Dimensions: 12.7 x 1.6 x 20.3 cm

Lightning Source UK Ltd.
Milton Keynes UK
UKHW012335060319
338640UK00001B/36/P

9 781916 021754